MW01234546

# An Unexpected Ally

**Strangers and Second Chances, Volume 2**

Meg Osborne

Published by Meg Osborne, 2021.

This is a work of fiction. Similarities to real people, places, or events are entirely coincidental.

AN UNEXPECTED ALLY

**First edition. April 30, 2021.**

Written by Meg Osborne.

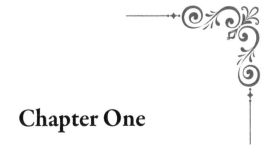

# Chapter One

"I have heard a rumour about you..."

Colonel Richard Fitzwilliam flinched when he recognised the sound of George Wickham's lazy drawl over the noise of other drinkers at the Meryton inn favoured by the men of his barracks.

It had become Richard's habit of late to find time most days to pass a quiet half an hour nursing a mug of weak ale and making conversation with whichever of the men chanced to surround him. It served him well, for the difficulty of assuming control of a band of men opposed to his arrival had lessened and he had begun to build something of a rapport with them. He grimaced, wishing that any of his other subordinates would choose this moment to come to him with a question, however complex and arduous to resolve if only to rescue him from Wickham's sly smile. No one came, so Richard met and matched his gaze, concealing his reluctance with a smile.

"Indeed? I wonder at people's lack of occupation if they choose me as a topic for their idle tongues."

"Then it is false?" Wickham set his glass down firmly on one corner of Richard's table and pulled up a chair, accepting an unoffered and unwarranted invitation to join him.

"Most probably." Richard took a sip of his drink, his eyes fixed on Wickham over the lip of the glass. "Rumours tend to be."

"Occasionally they are not," Wickham conceded, with a smile that betrayed secrets neither of them wished to revisit. "In this case...." He tilted his head to one side, surveying Richard with curiosity.

"You shall have to ask me outright, Wickham, I am in no mood for games this evening and too tired to have confidences teased out of me." He sighed, raking a hand through his hair and thinking wearily of the pile of reports he had yet to read through before he could begin to think of retiring that evening. His mind taunted him, accurately, that if he had spent fewer hours at Longbourn and more attending to his regimental responsibilities over the past few days he might be in a better position that evening. His cheeks warmed, for he could not help but think he had made the right decision. *What is a pile of reports compared to love?* He scoffed at his own nonsense, glad that none of his men - and above all George Wickham - were privy to the sentimentality that had invaded his thoughts.

"Very well." Wickham's expression had changed, such that it took Richard a moment to confirm to himself that his friend could not read his mind. Somehow, he seemed to sense the contents of his thoughts all the same. His sly grin grew, making Richard uncomfortable.

"You are to be married."

"I am -" Richard choked on the mouthful of weak ale he had taken in an attempt to hide from Wickham's probing gaze. He coughed, clearing his lungs before responding. "I am to be married. That is the rumour, is it? Well." He raked his hand through his hair a second time, dishevelling it further.

"Then it is not true? You have not been making frequent calls at a certain house? Paying your attentions to the eldest and most beautiful of all the sisters - arguably the most beautiful young lady in all of Meryton?"

Richard swallowed a curse, seeing there would be no denying the truth. Wickham had gleaned it from somewhere, even if he exaggerated about the matter being the talk of Meryton.

"It is true I have called there on occasion," he equivocated. "That is not a revelation. You accompanied me there yourself. Mr Bennet and I have become friends. We play chess."

"And you take long walks with Miss *Jane* Bennet." Wickham reached across the table and slapped Richard on the shoulder, hard. "Come, Fitzwilliam! Do not act as this were some great secret you must keep quiet on the pain of death. It matters little to me if you should marry her. I would be a trifle more vexed, should you have set your cap at Elizabeth, but..."

Richard frowned, recalling the rapport he had noticed between Wickham and Elizabeth and wondering at it. He had dismissed it at first, certain that George Wickham was merely being George Wickham, charming any young lady who happened to catch his eye. Now he wondered if, truthfully, Elizabeth Bennet *had* caught his eye, and if his game with her was more than the transient display of charm he offered most young ladies of short acquaintance.

"I did not realise you thought so highly..."

"Because I do not find myself there every moment I am spared from my duties, you mean?" Wickham chuckled, swallowing the rest of his drink and summoning another. He grew serious. "I am a little less welcome than you, for Mr Bennet has no desire in courting me for a chess companion." His voice dropped. "Or for a son."

Richard frowned, wondering, not for the first time, how Wickham came across his information, and how he so often succeeded in being unerring in its application.

"Family disapproval as never stopped you before," Richard muttered, grimly, feeling a strange compulsion to remind Wickham, however obliquely, that he had not forgotten their shared history, even if the fates had forced them now into a tense kind of friendship. He had not forgotten it, nor had he forgiven Wickham for the trauma he wrought on poor Georgiana. *I am hardly inclined to stand by and watch you do so a second time!*

"True," Wickham conceded. "But this time...it is different. Elizabeth Bennet is unlike any young lady I have met before and knowing her...perhaps I might even say I am a changed man." He shrugged, affecting an unreadable smile. "I dare say my long stint in His Majesty's Regiment has reformed me. As has your sterling supervision." He saluted Richard with his empty glass. "I am glad we are friends again, Fitzwilliam, and if you *are* poised to win the delicate Jane Bennet's hand for your very own, perhaps you will not forget to put in a good word for me with her sister." His eyes glinted dangerously. "And recall that I know shadows from your past just as well as you know mine. It would serve us both ill to drag them out into the light, wouldn't it?"

Richard said nothing and a moment later Wickham was hailed from the corner of the inn, where a small group of soldiers were poised to begin a card game. With a smile, Wickham got to his feet, punching Richard lightly on the arm as he passed him, and joined the group to a roar of welcome. Richard barely noticed, his gaze fixed, unseeing, on the middle distance.

That was Wickham's game, then. He had helped Richard gain status and security within the regiment knowing his own past would stay buried: Richard could not risk sharing it without harming Georgiana. Now, he wished for Richard to smooth the obstacles in his personal life as well, or he would destroy them both.

*Can I do it? Condemn another young lady to the fate Georgiana so narrowly escaped? After all, it was my fault the pair ever even met one another, and my fault that things escalated as they did...*

Another volley of laughter reached him from the corner of the pub and his stomach turned. He stood, leaving his drink half-drunk, and made his way back to the barracks, feeling in need of quiet rather than company, and hoping that in doing so he might puzzle himself out of the unfortunate allegiance that had ensnared him.

*DEARLY BELOVED, WE are gathered here today...*

Jane Bennet's blue eyes grew cloudy as she allowed her imagination to run wild, picturing the most perfect of spring days. Her hair would be curled just so, pinned in place and decorated with flowers. She would wear a beautiful dress, chosen specially for the occasion, and beside her would stand...

"Mr Darcy?"

Jane flinched, spinning away from the looking glass to glare at Lizzy who burst into her room without knocking, pausing for a moment with a merry laugh.

"What are you doing?"

"Nothing," Jane said, crossly, letting go of the hair she held in place and smoothing away some imagined creases in her dress. "Don't you knock?"

"Not always." Lizzy bounded in, landing on the bed with a thump. "You were daydreaming." Her eyes danced with amusement. "Admit it! You were daydreaming about your wedding day." She sighed, clutching her hands to her breast in an affectation of romance. "Oh, how beautiful I will look, with my hair pinned just so, surrounded by spring flowers and with the Colonel Fitzwilliam beside me..."

"Hush!" Jane tossed a pillow at her sister, the heat in her cheeks intensifying with the accuracy of Lizzy's speculations. *Am I so easy to read?* She perched opposite her, eager to change the subject.

"What were you saying about Mr Darcy?"

"Oh, nothing." Lizzy hugged the pillow to her, burying her head into it so that when she spoke, her voice was muffled. "Merely that Father has been corresponding with him."

"Oh?" Jane frowned. "I did not realise they were friends."

"No more did I!" Lizzy groaned, and when she lifted her head, her features folded into a scowl. "I do not believe they are, merely that Mr Darcy must forever poke his nose into everybody else's business, even when he is not in Hertfordshire! He still seems to think everything that happens here is of his chief concern, though we all remain, of course, far beneath his notice."

If Jane was concerned about the transparency of her own feelings, Lizzy seemed oblivious to hers, her agitation about Mr Darcy's interference - if that was truly what was behind his letters to Mr Bennet - proving nothing more than that she thought of him often. Jane turned this thought over in her mind, wondering how she had not noticed it before.

"What?" Lizzy straightened. "What *hmm?* You are thinking, Jane. I do not like it."

"That is the pot calling the kettle black!" Jane retorted, reaching for her pillow before Lizzy continued squashing it flat. "I merely reflected that it is quite interesting how often you succeed in mentioning Mr Darcy's name, despite claiming still to care absolutely nothing for him and thinking of him even less. As you say, he has been absent from Meryton for quite some time now and has not yet faded from your memory."

"He will be absent no longer!" Lizzy replied, trying to appear unconcerned and only slightly succeeding. "That is what I came to tell you. Papa has had word that he is returning to Netherfield."

Jane's eyes widened, her question answered before she even had a chance to formulate it.

"Alone." Lizzy frowned. "I do not know what has become of Mr Bingley. And it is but a fleeting visit."

"You seem to have deduced a great deal of news from Papa's correspondence," Jane remarked, striving to keep her voice and her features neutral. "I am surprised he was willing to share as much."

"He may have left the letter out on the side for anyone to read...." Lizzy confessed, tracing a line of embroidery on Jane's quilt. She glanced up, two pinpricks of colour dotting her cheeks as she grinned. "Anyone of an enquiring disposition, anyway."

"Which means you." Jane sighed.

"Don't lecture, Janey! If I had not read the letter, we should not know that Mr Darcy is to grace us with his presence once more. Now that we do know it, we can plan our next steps."

"What next steps?" Jane stood, turning back to the mirror and returning to the task of pinning her hair up, which had been sacrificed for a moment's idle daydreaming before Lizzy burst in. "You still claim you want nothing to do with the man."

"It cannot be nothing," Lizzy remarked, with a philosophical shrug that might have convinced someone who did not know her as well as Jane did. "Not if you are set to marry his cousin!"

"Lizzy!" Jane scolded, turning to check that the door to her room was closed and Lizzy's comment couldn't have been overheard. "I told you that in confidence!"

"I know." Elizabeth's smile dimmed just a fraction. "But it can't be very long until it is common knowledge, surely? How long before Colonel Fitzwilliam speaks to Papa? I am surprised it is not already all agreed." She frowned. "I hope he is not playing some game..."

"He is not!" Jane insisted, colouring at the thought. How could she explain to her sister that it was she, not Richard, who delayed speaking to Papa? He would have the whole thing arranged and settled already, had she permitted him to. It was what she wanted, wasn't it? Why then did she delay matters?

"He is to dine here this evening," Lizzy said, her eyes already bright with a plan. "I am sure he will speak of it then. I guarantee it! Oh, how exciting, Jane! A wedding is just precisely what this family needs! What a welcome home it will be for Mary!"

# Chapter Two

"You are sure your parents expect you home today?"

Fitzwilliam Darcy had asked the question already but he still did not feel entirely satisfied by Mary Bennet's mute nod, as the carriage they both occupied trundled slowly towards Hertfordshire.

"And they know that I am accompanying you?"

"I thought you wrote," Mary remarked, looking up from the book that she had been bent over for the duration of the journey thus far. "To tell them as much."

"Quite so." Darcy nodded. "I did."

Still, his nerves would not settle. It was not making such a journey in near silence, for silence rarely if ever troubled him. It was not even sharing such close quarters with Mary Bennet, for since witnessing the growing friendship between her and Georgiana he had found himself thinking of her as almost a second sister. Georgiana's company with them, indeed, might have elevated the short journey from tolerable to enjoyable, but Darcy had been bound and determined to prevent that. He would not risk Georgiana's coming to Hertfordshire, to be once more in such close proximity to George Wickham. How he would endeavour to keep her from it once news of their cousin's approaching wedding reached her, he didn't know.

*The wedding.*

He leaned one elbow against the door, resting his chin in his palm and allowing his eyes to close. He had never conceived of such a thing. How could he, when he still found it strangeness itself that of all the regiments in England his cousin Richard should find himself in charge of the one based at Meryton? Stranger still, that he should meet and lose his heart to Jane Bennet in so short and swift a time frame.

*I cannot blame him entirely for that*, he conceded. Had Charles Bingley's heart not been lost just as swiftly and completely? *Was not my own?*

Not to Jane Bennet, of course, and he might have concealed the matter quite successfully from his friends, but to himself, Darcy was no stranger. He had lost his heart to Elizabeth Bennet the first moment he laid eyes on her, much as Charles had done with her sister. Regardless of any pointed dismissal he had offered Charles Bingley, and despite his most ardent of hopes, the development seemed to have ben permanent. His visit to Longbourn was, on the face of it, a gentleman's duty to escort a young woman of his acquaintance safely home. That he might subsequently discover the truth of the rumours about Jane Bennet's engagement - his cousin's engagement, if this was indeed the case, for Richard had certainly not sent word by his own pen - was an errand he undertook for his friend. But his motivation for travelling back to Hertfordshire, when he had once planned never to set foot there again, was the chance to see Elizabeth Bennet again.

*Fool.* What had his separation from her taught him if not that love did nought but cause trouble? Charles was a wreck of a man at the thought that Jane Bennet had formed an attachment to someone else. Richard was destined for heartbreak, for Darcy thought it highly likely that Jane would jilt him for Bingley given even the slightest indication he still cared. And he, Darcy, was somehow caught between his oldest friend and his cousin! There could be no easy resolution.

*So I would do well to guard my own heart against any further entanglement with the Bennet family*, he reminded himself, knowing full well that his heart was too foolish to listen. He had once prided himself on the degree of self-control he possessed but that was being tested every hour and found wanting. Perhaps it was not self-will Darcy was endowed with but merely a lack of suitable temptation.

"Mr Darcy?"

Mary's voice was slight, raised just enough that he might hear it over the clatter of carriage wheels, and he lifted his head, surprised to find her sharp eyes fixed on him.

"Is something the matter, Miss Mary?"

"I was about to ask you the same thing." She closed her book, hugging it close to her chest and allowing her chin to rest on its edge. "You seem troubled."

"No," Darcy said, shortly, tempering his gruffness only when he saw her features fall. "I am quite well." He paused. "Thank you." He turned away, watching the scenery surrounding them change as they took the now-familiar road to Longbourn. What mercy! He would be spared any further consideration by the bird-like Miss Mary who was a great deal more insightful than he had ever credited her with being.

"Here we are," he remarked, praying his delight at being spared a long journey was not too obvious. "You are home, Miss Mary."

She tore her eyes away from him, at last, to peer out of the window, nodding in a quiet acknowledgement as they slowed to a stop.

"You are not pleased?" He could not help but notice the shadow that settled on her pale features and was not easily shaken off.

"Of course I am." Her words were mechanical, lacking the lilting music that came to her voice in the hundred conversations he had witnessed her have with Georgiana in the past few days.

Curious, yet disinclined to press her, Darcy climbed out, determined to escort her to the door whilst the driver brought her cases. Mary seemed to shrink with every step they took towards Longbourn's looming frontage, but before Darcy could consider the matter in any greater detail, the door flew open.

"Miss Mary!"

Their housekeeper, at least, was delighted to see her, and Mary brightened considerably at this, setting Darcy a little more at ease. He poised to leave, hesitating a moment too long before going, as a movement inside the house caught his eyes and the one woman in all England he could never keep from his thoughts for long stepped out of a small room and into the corridor, directly into his line of sight.

"Miss Elizabeth!" He had called her name almost before he was aware of it, raising one arm in an awkward wave. "Good day."

"Mr Darcy." Her voice was clipped, but he thought he detected the slightest of smiles on her face as she turned to look at him. "Do you intend on coming in to take tea? Or would you prefer we bring it to you in the doorway?"

SAFELY ENSCONCED IN her own personal corner of the Longbourn parlour, Lizzy peered over the top of her teacup towards Mr Darcy, who seemed easily as out of place to be sitting amidst a gaggle of Bennets as he ever had.

"How kind of you to bring our Mary home safely, Mr Darcy!" Mrs Bennet gushed, looking quite teary at the degree of care he had taken.

"It was no trouble, Mrs Bennet." His grimace approached a smile, and he busied himself with taking a sip of his tea. "I was poised to make the journey anyhow."

"Where will you be staying?" Lydia asked, never one to stand on ceremony when there was the possibility of gossip. "Did Mr Bingley come with you?"

This was accompanied by a significant look from Lydia and Kitty at Jane, who appeared unmoved by the question. Lizzy, who knew her sister well, could see from the whiteness in her fingers how tightly Jane clasped her saucer and how much energy it cost her to appear so unaffected. She frowned. Ought it to matter to Jane whether or not Mr Bingley ever stepped foot in Hertfordshire again? She had found love with Colonel Fitzwilliam and was surely much happier with him than she ever might have been with Mr Bingley.

"Alas, no." Mr Darcy shifted uncomfortably on his chair. "He remains in London for - for now." He swallowed. "But he has given me free rein to stay at Netherfield while I am here."

"You must dine here this evening, in that case!" Mrs Bennet declared, glancing at her husband, who was seated contentedly in one corner of the room and taking no part in Mr Darcy's inquisition. "Mr Bennet!" she called, when his response was not forthcoming. "Tell Mr Darcy he must join us for dinner this evening."

"You must join us for dinner this evening." Mr Bennet offered a mechanical repetition of his wife's command. His lips quirked upwards into a smile. "If you can bear to. I shall endear you to the notion, somewhat, by advising you that your cousin, Colonel Fitzwilliam, will also be dining with us." His eyes twinkled over the top of his spectacles. "Perhaps that will enable you to endure further questioning."

"*Further questioning?*" Mrs Bennet's voice grew shrill, although she smiled. "How you do tease us, Mr Bennet! As if there is anything untoward about our taking a neighbourly interest in Mr Darcy, now that he is returned to us after so long away!"

"Mary was away also," Mr Bennet pointed out, turning to his middle daughter with a smile. "And she has yet to speak a word. Tell us, Mary, how was London?"

"Yes, tell us everything!" Kitty said, sliding her arm through Mary's and silently pledging her allegiance to the sister who had not spent all morning either teasing or criticising her. "Did you go to many assemblies? Who did you meet?"

"Oh, I'm sure I can answer that," Lydia shot back, a malicious gleam in her eye. She counted out the likely suspects on the fingers of one hand. "There were Aunt and Uncle Gardiner, the children, the servants..." Her gaze drifted towards their guest. "Oh, and Mr Darcy, of course."

"And my sister," Mr Darcy pointed out, shooting Mary an encouraging smile. "With whom you seemed to form quite the friendship. Tell them about yours and Georgiana's performance at dinner the other night, Mary."

This was a kindness quite unexpected - and from Mr Darcy, no less! Elizabeth could not help but warm to him for the notice he took of quiet, invisible Mary, nor deny the effect his invitation had. Mary blossomed, speaking more in that five minutes than she often did in a day, and succeeded in courting the attention of the whole room, who were as eager to know about Georgiana Darcy as they were to marvel over Mary's sudden transformation.

"She sounds nice, does not she?" Jane whispered, leaning close enough to Elizabeth that her comment might carry to no other ears but hers. "Miss Darcy. She was nought but a name to me before now, but it seems she and Mary became firm friends during their time together. I am pleased, for Mary could do with a companion."

Elizabeth nodded but again her eyes strayed to Mr Darcy. He ought to have seemed out of place at Longbourn, indeed he had never been there before without Mr Bingley to soften the ordeal. He was the same Mr Darcy, Lizzy knew, but there was something about him that seemed altogether different. Gone were the scowl and the sneer he so often wore to elevate himself above his neighbours. Indeed, he smiled, offering a word or two of agreement to Mary's tale, and at one point even laughed. Lizzy had never heard him laugh before, but the sound was so warm and uplifting that she found herself smiling in return.

"I see Miss Elizabeth agrees with me."

Her smile fell but too late. He had seen her smiling and now, when he looked at her, it was as if he had caught her unawares. She had no idea what it was she supposedly agreed with but could not dream of admitting as much.

"Yes," she said, hurriedly taking a sip of the tea that had grown lukewarm in her cup. "Yes, of course."

The conversation moved on and Elizabeth let out a sigh of relief at escaping further scrutiny until she felt Jane's suspicious gaze on her.

"You did not hear a word you just agreed to, did you?" Jane whispered, her lips quirking in amusement.

"I could hardly say I do not think Mary is a talented musician, could I?" Elizabeth shot back, praying that her guess was right. It was right enough, it seemed, for Jane rolled her eyes but let the matter drop and at last the occupants of the parlour lapsed into silence.

"Well!" Mr Darcy placed his cup down and got to his feet. "I must continue to Netherfield, or there is a chance I shall never make it."

"And you must come back here this evening!" Mrs Bennet reminded him. "Lizzy, you must persuade him! You are capable of persuading anyone into doing anything!"

Lizzy flushed and Lydia let out a cackle of laughter, accompanied by a whispered comment Lizzy did not care to hear.

"I don't know about that -"

"Do not fret, Miss Elizabeth," Mr Darcy said, looking past her, although he spoke to her. "I shall take no further persuading. I confess the thought of eating alone in the cavernous Netherfield dining room does not sound entirely appealing after my day's journey." He turned to Mrs Bennet. "I very much appreciate the invitation and look forward to joining you this evening."

"Wonderful!" Mrs Bennet beamed, glowing pink under the light of Mr Darcy's gaze. "Wonderful."

"And for now, I shall take my leave." Mr Darcy bowed himself out of the room, and Lizzy noticed he had forgotten one glove. She considered herself for only a moment before leaping to her feet and snatching up the offending article and hurrying after their guest.

"Mr Darcy!"

He paused in the doorway, looking back at her with surprise and the hint of a smile that she was almost disappointed to offer him nothing more than his own mislaid glove.

"You forgot this."

"So I did." He was gruff once more, taking the glove with the smallest nods of thanks. "Actually, Miss Elizabeth..." He paused, peering past her as if to be sure he was not overheard. Lizzy's heart began to beat in her chest and for one wild moment she imagined it was not *Mr Darcy* whom she had spent the past several months despising standing before her, with the merest hint of a smile on his handsome face, but some gentlemanly *other*, some hero from a novel, poised to confess his love and alter the course of her life forever.

"Yes?" She shook herself out of her dream, swallowing past the lump in her throat. "Is there something the matter?"

Mr Darcy frowned, himself once again and Lizzy regretted her flight of fancy, wondering what had come over her that day that even Mr Darcy was rendered so agreeable.

"I do not know," he confessed, with an honesty that surprised them both. "I wonder -"

He peered past her again and all at once Elizabeth realised he was not wary of being overheard, but wary of being overheard *by Jane*. She felt a prickle of annoyance that even now he sought to cast aspersions on her sister's heart.

"It will surely be pleasant to be reunited with your cousin this evening, Mr Darcy. He has spoken of you a great deal."

This was not strictly true but it served to accomplish Lizzy's purpose. Mr Darcy straightened, growing serious.

"He has?"

"He has." Elizabeth smiled sweetly, her cheeks hurting with the effort it took to hold the expression in place. "He has called here often. I am sure you are aware of the friendship that has blossomed between him and my sister. Indeed!" She shrugged her shoulders, smiling still wider and ignoring the pain. "You will be able to witness it for yourself this evening. You will find, I am sure, that they make a delightful couple. Good day, Mr Darcy!"

Bidding him farewell with a brightness she did not feel, Lizzy turned and made her way back into the parlour to rejoin her family.

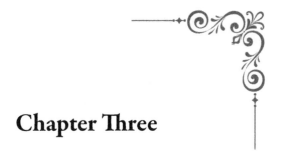

# Chapter Three

Whilst Netherfield had never really been "home" to Darcy, it felt even less warm and welcoming than ever before as he strode along the deserted corridors to reacquaint himself with his new temporary lodgings.

He was grateful to Charles for offering it to him, although he felt a little awkward at forcing the staff to reopen everything for the sake of one inhabitant. Catching sight of their housekeeper, he paused a moment to advise her that as he was only to be staying - alone - for a few days, he would like her to reassure the staff that they need go to no particular trouble on his account.

"Oh!" He turned, catching her before she scurried away. "And I shall be dining at Longbourn this evening, so please advise the kitchen that there is no need to prepare a meal."

"Very good, Mr Darcy," she murmured, dipping in a curtsey before hurrying off.

Darcy straightened, making his way to the parlour and shivering a little. Despite the bright spring weather, there was still a chill in the air and he strode over to the fireplace, where a meagre measure of coals fed a few feeble flames. Reaching for the poker, he agitated the embers, getting a little more heat that warmed him but was still not conducive to comfort.

Abandoning the attempt and feeling strangely perturbed to be so unsettled by isolation, Darcy made his way towards the stables, borrowing one of Netherfield's horses and riding the short distance to Meryton, thinking he would find some gift he might bring to Longbourn that evening. Some spring flowers for Mrs Bennet, perhaps, or something sweet the family might share.

Darcy was naturally generous, although he lacked friends upon whom to dote, and his errands cheered him so that he was soon laden down by flowers, a bottle of brandy and all manner of foodstuffs sufficient that he was forced to place the whole lot into a crate and send it on ahead of him, for he would never manage to carry it on his horse. He scratched out a brief note for Mr and Mrs Bennet, thanking them for their hospitality and sending a token of his appreciation before this evening's meal, and continued on his way, not quite ready to return home to the empty shell of Netherfield Park.

He was not aware of it but by some coincidence, his feet took him on a circuitous route past the regimental barracks, and he found himself scanning the crowd of milling red-coats for his cousin.

*Richard is, after all, my reason for being here*, he reminded himself. He would appreciate the chance to speak to his cousin alone before they were thrust together once again in front of an audience.

"Darcy?"

Richard had spotted him first and Darcy turned, surprised and pleased that he would not have to go to any greater lengths to find him.

"I thought that was you! What on earth are you doing here?" Richard smiled as he walked, reaching Darcy just in time to greet him properly, with a warm handshake. His smile dimmed a little. "Georgiana is not with you." It was not quite a question.

Darcy shook his head.

"I thought it prudent she stay in London. I do not plan on being here long." He forced a smile, wishing he could feel a fraction of the ease Richard seemed to embody. "I came to escort Miss Mary Bennet home. When I heard she would be making the journey alone it seemed only right to ensure she travelled safely. And I have an errand or two to attend to on Bingley's behalf. I wonder if I can persuade you to walk with me for a quarter-hour. It is so long since we saw each other, Cousin, and -"

"Unfortunately not." Richard sighed, rubbing his chin thoughtfully. "But I can spare you a few minutes if you are not averse to spending them in my room?" He clutched a handful of papers. "I must take these inside and remain where I may be found." He rolled his eyes. "The delights of running a regiment, I can't begin to tell you. Come, walk with me."

Darcy fell into step beside him, allowing his cousin to escort him through the rambling barracks and through a heavy door to a small room containing a desk and a few chairs, and with a roaring fire in the hearth.

"Excellent, they must have known we were coming." Richard chuckled, dropping his pile of papers on the desk and pausing a moment before the fire to absorb its heat. "You'll take a brandy?" He reached for the bottle and poured two glasses without waiting for Darcy's response. "Here." He passed him a glass, taking a sip from his own and grimacing. "It can't compete with your usual, but -"

"It's fine." Darcy swallowed half of it in one bitter gulp. "Thank you."

Richard sank heavily into his chair and Darcy feigned interest in a framed landscape on the wall. He was not unaware of Richard's scrutiny, so it did not come as a complete surprise when his cousin raised a question in his direction.

"So why are you here? There must be some reason, especially if you are here alone."

Darcy took a long moment to respond, taking another sip of his drink and turning back to meet his cousin's gaze.

"I came to see you," he said at last, selecting a chair opposite Richard and folding himself carefully into it. "You could hardly expect me not to make the journey when I knew you were here. It is not far."

"I see." Richard steepled his fingers, leaning his chin into them.

"And..." Darcy sighed, realising there would be no way to have this conversation without actually having it. "I hear congratulations are in order." He lifted his glass in a show of a salute. "It seems you are to be married."

Richard laughed, a slow, grim laugh, so unlike his usual that Darcy frowned.

"Am I misinformed?"

"You are...informed." Richard leaned back in his chair, shaking his head in disbelief. "It seems the whole world is cognizant of my plans before I am even certain of them myself."

Darcy surveyed his cousin carefully. Then...all of this was a mistake? He could not be so fortunate.

"But you and Miss Bennet -"

"I have asked her to marry me," Richard said, nodding slowly. "I have asked and she has accepted." He could not keep his lips from curving upwards into a smile. "Although we have yet to mention it to her parents. Mr and Mrs Bennet..."

"Are sure to agree." Darcy had never seen his cousin hesitant about a single thing in his life: it was this that had driven him into the regiment, and this that had gained him rank, fortune, reputation.

"I'm glad you think so." Richard grinned. "I had planned to ask them tonight."

WATCHING MARY SPEAK about London, Jane almost wished she had been there. She missed the hustle and bustle of the town, and when she imagined the balls, the assemblies, the concerts and lectures that Mary spoke of with undisguised enthusiasm, she could not help but feel a pang of envy.

"And Mr Bingley? How is he?"

It was Mrs Bennet who asked this, oblivious to the sharp glare she received from both Elizabeth and Mary for asking such a question in Jane's hearing. Swallowing against a lump in her throat, Jane forced herself to play peacemaker, speaking his name for the first time in what felt like forever.

"Yes, how is Mr Bingley? And Miss Bingley? I am sure you saw a great deal of them and Mr Darcy. Do tell us how our friends fare, Mary."

*Our friends.* That made it sound as if Mr Bingley was almost nothing to her now. *As he is.* She wished only that she might persuade herself as easily as the rest of her family.

"Oh, well enough," Mary said, with an airiness to her voice that made the statement seem true. Yes, Jane could imagine Mr Bingley was *well enough* and *happy enough* and *busy enough* in London. It had certainly seemed that way, in the few words she had received from Caroline Bingley. *He has forgotten me entirely.* The fact that Mr Darcy should return now, without him, must surely only solidify that fact.

*And I am pleased*, Jane thought, willing herself to smile as Mary conjured another image of London's many bustling parks. She *was* pleased. She nursed a secret - not truly a secret, for Lizzy knew it and she suspected, from the way Mary's dark eyes continued to rest on her, before bouncing away again only to return, that if she did not know the fact of Jane's informal engagement she surely suspected it. She knew of Colonel Fitzwilliam, at least, and of his regular calls at Longbourn.

"But I am sure life here has not been at a standstill," Mary said at last, when she had grown tired of the incessant questioning of her family. "Jane? Lizzy?"

"Of course you only imagine Lizzy and Jane to have things to tell!" Lydia sniffed, with a bitter toss of her head. "Don't you care at all for what Kitty and I have been doing in all this time we were away? You might have written!"

"I did!" Mary protested, looking wounded. "I wrote to all of you! Lizzy was the only one who made efforts to respond, so in the end, I addressed myself to her." She glanced around the room. "I did tell her the news was to be shared."

"I liked your letters," Kitty said, in a surprising show of solidarity. She had missed Mary more than anyone might have expected her to. "Although I do wish I might have been asked to go. I have only been to London -"

"Jane has news!" Lydia remarked, eagerly silencing her sister and becoming the centre of the conversation in one easy movement. She shot a wicked grin at her sister. "Don't you?"

"Not really." Jane could feel her cheeks colouring and looked down at her embroidery that she had been clinging to, without actually working on, for the past quarter-hour. "Nothing worth sharing."

Lydia sighed dramatically before leaning forward and beginning, in a stage-whisper designed to antagonise her sister, to describe to Mary the latest happenings at Longbourn.

"Colonel Fitzwilliam has been calling her ever so often. I wonder if Lizzy ever thought to mention that in her letters."

Lizzy was studiously avoiding everyone's gaze, so studiously that it caught Jane's attention and she turned to Mary, who did not seem in the slightest bit surprised by Lydia's revelations.

"She mentioned it." Mary looked at Jane. "I gather he is very agreeable and engaging, although of course, I have that from Georgiana." She smiled. "Who is a little biased."

"Oh, we are all biased where Colonel Fitzwilliam is concerned," Mrs Bennet remarked from the settee where she had been happily dozing and listening to the chatter of her daughters. "He is ever so agreeable! Far more so than his cousin, although -"

"Mama!"

Mrs Bennet shrugged her shoulders.

"I do not see why I should be criticised for stating a fact. It is only my opinion that Mr Darcy is less agreeable than his cousin, although I am sure you will all agree with me..."

"Mama, a thing is either a fact or an opinion, it cannot be both," Lizzy said, quietly. She was flushing a deep and brilliant red, but none of the sisters, save for Jane, seemed to have noticed. She kicked her discreetly, which made Elizabeth look at her, but before she could query the change in her countenance, Mrs Bennet had spoken again, her voice taking on a shrill, self-pitying tone she favoured when she felt ill-used by her daughters.

"Very well, it is *my opinion*, which clearly counts for nothing in the eyes of certain members of this family, that Colonel Fitzwilliam is quite the most agreeable and most charming - not to mention handsome - gentleman of our acquaintance. I shall endeavour not to say anything bad about Mr Darcy, and I suppose it must be acknowledged that he seemed a good deal more amiable this afternoon than I recall him being in the past..."

"He was very kind to escort me back from London," Mary piped up, eager to praise her benefactor. "And his sister is so very agreeable -"

"Ugh! If you are going to wax lyrical about the *divine Miss Darcy* again I am going to go upstairs," Lydia groaned, hauling herself to her feet. "Anyone would think you had never had a friend before, Mary!"

Mary said nothing, but Jane thought it entirely possible that there was a degree of truth to Lydia's teasing.

"I am pleased to hear that she is agreeable, Mary," Jane said, eager to comfort her sister in the best way she could. "What a pity she could not be persuaded to accompany her brother back with you, that we might know her as well."

"It is a shame," Mary agreed. "She was quite eager to come, but Mr Darcy would not hear of it." She shrugged her thin shoulders. "He insisted that he had business to attend to and would not be here for very long..." She trailed off, looking at Elizabeth, who had sniffed and tossed her head as if wishing for this particular part of their conversation to end.

"I do not see why he bothered to come back at all, in that case!" she remarked, her eyes flashing with something that might have been annoyance. "He had already caused such upheaval by leaving in the first place, why come back again at all?"

# Chapter Four

Once welcomed into Longbourn, Richard strolled quickly down the corridor towards the parlour but before he reached it, he turned left, knocking once on the door to a different room and opening it at the sound of a quick, quiet, "yes".

"Jane!" He smiled to see her standing, silhouetted in the firelight that made the small library dance with shadows. "You got my note?"

Jane nodded, reaching for him and they embraced. Parting, Richard offered her his arm.

"Shall we go now? Your father will be in his study, I suppose?"

Jane nodded.

"I made sure of it." She bit her lip, and Richard frowned, concerned to see her mood slip from happiness so soon. "Do you think it is right to tell him now? Like this?"

"You would prefer I made a formal speech at dinner?" Richard chuckled. "Present my petition to a panel including your mother and each of your sisters in turn. I see, I am to earn my prize."

"No!" Jane elbowed him sharply in the side and he feigned agony before a mock-severe look from his fiancée forced him into seriousness. "But if Father does not approve..."

"You think he won't approve?" Richard's voice was bright, still, warm and teasing, but he could not quite conceal the fear that turned his stomach at the thought of Mr Bennet refusing his suit. What right had he to ask for Jane Bennet's hand? He had a small fortune - very small, if he was honest - and whilst his family was old and established and tenuously connected to older and more established families yet, that did not mean a great deal where the promise of a future home was concerned. He straightened, swallowing against a lump in his throat and reached for the door. "Let us ask him, Jane. His response is out of our control, and we have waited long enough."

*I have waited long enough* was what he truly wished to say. He had wanted to speak of their engagement long before this evening, but the timing was never right. Jane wished to keep the secret a fraction longer. As had been Richard's fear, the secret was ill-kept, and it occurred to him, with Darcy's arrival and apparent foreknowledge of the event, that they ran the very real risk of Mr Bennet hearing of the match from lips other than his own, which would do more damage than even the meanest of suits.

"Very well," Jane whispered, and they exchanged one last kiss - for luck - before venturing back along the quiet corridor and knocking gently on the door to Mr Bennet's study.

"Come!" called the familiar voice of the Bennet patriarch, who looked up from his desk and beamed when he saw his visitor. "Richard! You have come early!" His eyes twinkled behind his spectacles. "Think we can sneak in a chess match before dinner? A fine plan! Very fine! I ought to have considered it myself. Ah, Jane! How pretty you look this evening..." He trailed off, seeing how closely the pair stood together and making sense of the tableau even without the need for any further explanation. "Ah." His brow furrowed as he saw the chances of a chess game slipping away, and he leaned back in his chair, gesturing to the two to join him.

"Mr Bennet," Richard began, unwilling and unable to wait any longer before finding out whether the future he had begun to dream of, to prize and value amongst all others, would be allowed to him or not. "I am sure you have already guessed what I - what we - have come to speak to you about, but I will make this brief." He smiled. "I confess I am incapable of making grand speeches."

"And I am not generally in favour of hearing them." Mr Bennet affixed a patient expression to his features, although the twinkle had not entirely gone from his eyes, from which Richard took some encouragement. "Proceed."

"I wish to marry your daughter, sir. Jane and I have come to know each other a little over the past few weeks and I think - that is, we think - that we should like very much to spend the rest of our lives together. I have a little fortune, far smaller, I confess, than I should like to offer, but I am gainfully employed." He grimaced. "And am assured of there being a continued need for me in His Majestys Regiment as long as I am willing to serve." He paused. "And I am willing. I can provide a home for Jane and I assure you that it would be the happiest home imaginable, for it would be filled with love and friendship..."

There was a long moment of silence and Richard racked his brains, wondering what else he could say that might better plead his case.

"And space enough to welcome guests?" Mr Bennet asked, at last. "For I assure you, if you and Jane set up home somewhere - anywhere - my wife will insist upon us visiting two, three, four times a year. She may well want to move us there permanently."

It took Richard a moment to recognise, from the twinkle in Mr Bennet's eyes and the low rumble in his throat that this was an attempt at humour, and, partly out of relief, he laughed, nodding enthusiastically as he caught Jane's eye and laughed louder.

"Yes, there will be space to welcome guests for as long as they care to come. You may even help us choose the house, to ensure it is to your liking."

"My dear Richard, I should not dream of saying such a thing within my wife's hearing, for fear of her taking you up on it." Mr Bennet's gaze slid from Richard to Jane, his smile dimming just a fraction. "Well, Jane? Is this what you wish for your future? You know that to be married to a colonel of such reputation will not necessarily be an easy road to tread."

Richard felt Jane's hand flinch a little in the crook of his elbow and he covered it with his free hand, a swift, silent encouragement. *I am going nowhere*, the gesture told her. *Have no fear. You will never lose me.*

"Yes," Jane whispered, nodding once, twice in quick succession. "Yes, this is what I want."

"Then who am I to stand in the way of it?" Mr Bennet exclaimed, standing up and sending more than one pile of papers cascading to the floor in his enthusiasm to gather his eldest daughter and soon-to-be son-in-law into a warm embrace. "We must celebrate! Ah! I hear the door. That must be our other guest arriving. Come, come! Do not let's hide away the evening in here. There must be a toast, and my wife must be told." He winced, looking longingly towards his desk before shaking his head. "And I suppose I must be there to hear her delighted squeals." Drawing a fortifying breath, he urged the pair to precede him out into the corridor. "Come, come. Let us announce it at once, and let the celebrations begin!"

DARCY HAD TIMED HIS arrival at Longbourn to perfection, knocking on the door at precisely the time he was instructed to come, yet it seemed when the door was opened and he was ushered indoors, that a celebration was already in full swing.

"Mr Darcy!" Mrs Bennet was the first to spot him, marching over to take him by the arm and physically drag him into the parlour that reverberated with laughter and merriment. "Mr Darcy! What news! Your cousin has proposed to our dear Jane and she has consented to marry him!"

"Indeed?" Darcy's gaze went straight to Richard seeking confirmation but the abject delight on his ordinarily stoical cousin's face outstripped the need for a word. "Well, then I congratulate you." He turned to the rest of the family. "All of you. Miss Bennet." He bowed to Jane. "I wish you very happy."

"Thank you." Her voice was tremulous and barely audible, but Darcy put that down to delight at her happy state and turned to embrace his cousin with rather less formality.

"Sorry," Richard muttered, close enough that his words would not carry. "I couldn't wait any longer, and you see? I need not have hesitated!"

Darcy said nothing but accepted the glass of brandy that Mr Bennet thrust towards him.

"We shall toast the happy couple now, and then again after dinner." His eyes sparkled with merriment. "Especially as you were kind enough to provide us with the means."

"Yes, Mr Darcy! I almost forgot to thank you for the kind basket you sent."

"It was nothing." Darcy was a little embarrassed to be so singled out in the sight of such delight. What was a parcel of foodstuffs in light of an engagement? Nursing his drink, he allowed the family to circle Jane and Richard again, taking a slow step back and finding safety in a quiet corner.

"You do not approve."

This was not a question. It was barely even a comment and Darcy looked to his right in surprise to see that Elizabeth Bennet had somehow materialised there.

"I?"

"Oh, Mr Darcy. You must not choose now to become discreet." Elizabeth continued to smile and applaud the very tearful and longwinded speech her mother was making, the words she directed to Darcy spoken in such a low voice that he was not sure at first that he did not imagine them.

"Discreet?" He took a sip of his brandy.

"You have never shied away from saying precisely what you think about this family. You must not do so now!"

Darcy's heart sank. She referenced the slight, again. Would he never be free of that? He had spoken out of turn, he acknowledged that. He had certainly never expected his words to be overheard and turned against him at every opportunity thereafter.

"I wish them very happy," he said, with a shrug of one shoulder. "Can you say the same?"

This frank question seemed to be enough to bring Elizabeth to a standstill. Her breath caught and she appeared to be truly considering the question before at last turning to him with a smile that made him wish was intended for him.

"Yes, Mr Darcy. I wish them very happy." She turned back to her family. "Well, oughtn't we to go to dinner? Or do you plan to spend the whole evening standing around the parlour?"

"Quite right, quite right!" Mr Bennet began swiftly to orchestrate matters and the procession into dinner began, but before Darcy was able to take Elizabeth's arm, as he steeled himself to do, Lydia Bennet appeared.

"You will escort me, Mr Darcy. You do not mind it, do you?" She pulled on his arm and he felt quite unable to refuse, especially when he saw Lizzy laugh and take Jane's other side so that she walked three-abreast with the new couple.

"Very well," he said, grimly. "And how do you fare, Miss Lydia?"

"Oh *dreadfully!*" Lydia sighed, looking and sounding at that moment every inch her mother's daughter.

"You are not happy about the prospect of a wedding?"

"I would be if it were mine!" Lydia grinned. "Although I suppose I cannot fault Jane's choices too strongly. Your cousin will be just about bearable as a brother."

"He will be delighted to hear it."

"I do think it a shame poor Wickham could not be here this evening, though!"

Darcy stiffened. *Wickham?*

"He has called here often?"

"Oh, almost every time Colonel Fitzwilliam comes!" Lydia leaned conspiratorially close to Darcy. "They are good friends, you see, and of course he is so charming to us, always." She bristled. "Although Lizzy often tries to keep him to herself."

"Elizabeth?" Darcy strove to reorder his features so as not to betray his shock and disappointment at this detail. "Your sister is friends with Mr Wickham?"

"We all are!" Lydia insisted. "But he does spend far too long hovering around her. I think it frightfully unfair, for I am just as amiable a companion as she is, and far prettier. Don't you think so?"

She tilted her head to one side, peering up at him from beneath long lashes and affecting an expression she had clearly practised in a mirror.

"Charming," Darcy said, flatly. He was relieved when they reached the dining room and he was able to show Lydia to a chair beside her sisters, before seeking one for himself some distance away. With his gaze still on Lydia, he did not look as he sat down, so that it caught him by surprise to hear a muffled sigh and turn to see, too late to change his plans, that he had selected a chair immediately next to Elizabeth Bennet.

"We meet again," he said, with a grim smile.

"Anyone would think it was engineered that way," Elizabeth replied, with a polite smile. "I am surprised you do not prefer to sit with your cousin, Mr Darcy, although I suppose this offers a superior vantage point from which to pass judgment -"

"You seem to assume that I am in some way opposed to my cousin marrying your sister, Miss Elizabeth, when I have never said as much. Have I given even the slightest indication that I do not approve the match?"

"You did not approve of her marrying Mr Bingley," Elizabeth retorted, her eyes sparkling with malicious glee.

"How fortunate for all concerned, in that case, that she is not marrying Mr Bingley," Darcy muttered, reaching for his napkin and praying for strength to endure what was turning out to be a very challenging evening.

# Chapter Five

Meals at Longbourn had improved a little since Colonel Fitzwilliam had made it his habit to join them on occasion, and this evening's was no different, yet Elizabeth found her appetite lacking. She moved the food around on her plate in silence until she heard what sounded like laughter. Turning, she was surprised to see that Mr Darcy was smiling at the anecdote Colonel Fitzwilliam delivered with his characteristic humour and wit, and she rather regretted that she had missed the bulk of the story.

"...And so the whole thing worked out to my benefit, in the end." Colonel Fitzwilliam smiled, self-deprecatingly. "Although I could not have known it would at the time."

"As it has done with your meeting Jane," Mrs Bennet remarked, with a suspiciously tearful smile.

Elizabeth swallowed a sigh and turned back to her plate, but her reaction did not go unnoticed by Mr Darcy, who glanced at her, his features abruptly sinking into his more habitual expression of discontent.

"You do not share your mother's sentiments?" His words were low and shielded behind the hand that lifted his glass to his lips, so that it took Lizzy a moment to realise he had addressed a genuine question towards her. She glanced up, meeting his gaze and surprised to see curiosity burning in his dark eyes.

"I do not share my mother's emotion," she clarified, with a tight smile. "I care only that my sister is happy."

"And is she?"

This was a blunt question, and Lizzy was half-inclined to refuse it an answer. What right had Mr Darcy to enquire after Jane's happiness, as if he had ever cared to consider it when he wrenched Mr Bingley away from them? Yet, she reasoned, without Mr Bingley's absence there could have been no Colonel Fitzwilliam and certainly no engagement. She met Mr Darcy's gaze without blinking.

"Of course. She is engaged to marry a good man."

"But does she love him?" Darcy returned his glass to the table, setting down his cutlery and turning to face Elizabeth more directly. He leaned close enough that they might speak in whispers, safe in the knowledge that they would not be overheard by the rest of the table, who were now speculating wildly on the practicalities of the forthcoming wedding.

"You claim I do not approve of this match, that I did not approve of your sister's friendship with Charles Bingley. Perhaps you are right."

Lizzy's breath caught. Any one of a dozen vitriolic responses flooded her mind, but before she could offer a word of them, though, Mr Darcy had begun to speak again, his gaze pleading with her to allow him an explanation.

"I wished for my friend – as I wish for my cousin - to marry someone worthy of them. Someone who would love them."

His voice seemed to catch on the word *love* and Lizzy bit back the sharp retort that suggested Mr Darcy knew nothing of love. A light burned in his dark eyes that suggested this was not the case, and his protestations were not entirely ill-founded.

"My question, then, is whether your sister loves my cousin." He swallowed, reaching for his glass once more and wetting his lips before continuing. "I wish for them both to be happy, Elizabeth. *Both* of them. Do you not wish the same?"

"Of course." Lizzy's voice was constricted but she did not look away from him.

"Perhaps, then, we can work together."

"To part them?" Elizabeth gained confidence, her words rushing out in a sharp whisper that would have carried beyond their twosome had Lydia not chosen that moment to make a loud squeal about the likelihood of a foreign tour, once Jane and Colonel Fitzwilliam were married.

"You forget, Mr Darcy," Lizzy continued, in a subdued tone. "I am not Caroline Bingley. I care to see my sister happy _"

"Then you will care to ensure she marries for love. Nothing less than that."

Elizabeth frowned. Could this be Mr Darcy? Speaking of love as if it was all-important, all-consuming? She watched the shadows play across his features and wondered what had happened to change him in the short time they had been apart. She had convinced herself she knew Fitzwilliam Darcy well, understood completely his makeup and motivations. He had been back in her orbit for barely a day and everything she once thought a solid fact was cast into doubt.

"Jane is far more pragmatic than I," she began, wrenching her gaze away from his for some inexplicable fear that he might see beyond it to the truth she was not yet fully willing to share.

Mr Darcy was silent for a long moment before responding, and his answer, when it came, shocked Lizzy to her core.

"Does my cousin not deserve more than pragmatism upon which to build a future? Don't we all?"

"Darcy! What are you whispering about?"

Colonel Fitzwilliam's voice was jaunty and he called Darcy back to a conversation with Mr and Mrs Bennet and the rest of Elizabeth's sisters about an adventure in their shared youth at Pemberley. This was kindly done, for the mention of his estate gave Mr Darcy the confidence and enthusiasm to speak warmly and well, naming places and people he held in high esteem. Lizzy was silent, for once, eager to listen and learn more of the man she once thought she understood so completely.

*I was mistaken*, she realised, the remnants of her meal cooling untouched on her plate. She could not help but smile when Darcy told of climbing onto the roof of an outbuilding - Richard's idea, he was quick to insist - and the consequences that came when neither boy could climb down and a storm rolled in, leaving them exposed and soaked to the bone until at last a search party found them and brought both boys inside for comfort and punishment in equal measure.

"I am convinced our governess found the worst medicine she could find and made us drink double the draught we required so that we would not only recover without illness but also learn our lesson not to go adventuring in bad weather again."

The whole table laughed at this, even Lizzy, who was still smiling when Darcy turned back to meet her gaze, his eyes bright with amusement and affection and his features free - for once - of anything approaching a scowl.

RICHARD COULD NOT RECALL ever feeling so happy. Here, in Netherfield, he was surrounded by friends - by family - and he turned to Darcy as Mr Bennet poured all three gentlemen yet another generous measure of brandy.

"Well, what a fine evening for celebration this has turned into." Raising his glass, he saluted his soon-to-be son-in-law and took a hearty sip. "I suppose I must offer thanks to the absent Colonel Forster for bringing you here, to begin with!"

"Aye." Richard chuckled. "I shall tell him so myself when next we meet."

"How long are you to remain in post?"

Darcy's question was a genuine one, but something about his tone of voice made Richard's smile dim.

"My end date is not quite fixed." He nursed his drink, watching the light glint on the rippling surface of the amber liquor. "But I have leave enough accrued to be able to take some time to consider my plans." He shrugged. "I have felt for some time that military life has run its course for me. I have no desire to go back to the front, and at present it does not seem I am needed."

"No, indeed! You have done your part and earned some peace," Mr Bennet agreed. "Property, then. An estate." He eyed Darcy from behind his glasses. "Perhaps Netherfield Park will be open to you, as it does not seem as if its current tenants are eager to extend their lease."

Richard frowned. There was more to this question than logistics and living quarters. He watched his cousin shift uncomfortably in his seat, at last returning a question that was little more than a grunt.

"T'would suit, I am sure."

"I suppose you will write to your sister of the news," Mr Bennet continued, in that same unflinching tone that suggested he would not ask outright that which he wished to know but deduce it from words Darcy did not say. "She will be pleased, do you think?"

"Oh, undoubtedly." Darcy smiled, but he barely met Richard's gaze. "What lady is not delighted by the news of an engagement?"

Richard's lips quirked. He could think of ladies enough of his acquaintance who would not rejoice at the news of his marrying.

*At least I am not you, Darcy*, he thought, wordlessly watching his cousin as he took a sip of his drink. Their shared aunt, Lady Catherine de Bourgh, had made her plans for Darcy's future painfully clear. Were he to even think of forming a friendship - let alone marrying - someone who was not her own daughter Anne there would be hell to pay.

*She does not have the same preoccupation with my matrimonial future*, Richard mused, wondering if he ought to be offended by being given such freedom. His brother would not care either, except to remark that it was beyond time Richard settled down and embraced a more gentlemanly, settled lifestyle. *By which he would mean, of course, that he will no longer be expected to play host to me when I am between engagements.* The thought occurred to him then, as it had not done before, that he might, in marrying Jane and securing a home of his own, be spared the trouble of ever stepping foot across the threshold of his familial estate again. The thought was strangely sobering, and he did not realise how far his features had fallen until Mr Bennet remarked upon it.

"Why so glum, Richard? Here, have another drink." He had poured a second heavy measure before Richard could stop him, and he smiled briskly in gratitude.

"Not glum," he assured his companions. "Just reflecting for a moment." He took a sip of his brandy, grimacing at the burning sensation as he swallowed. "It is not every day one proposes, after all."

"I should hope not!" Mr Bennet chuckled, drinking his measure down and pouring another.

Only Darcy's glass remained three-quarters full. He was nursing it, not drinking it, which drew Richard's curiosity. The brandy was his gift, after all, and a fine vintage. His cousin was not particularly given to sobriety, particularly not when politeness dictated he drink, and this was a day of celebration, was it not?

Yet Darcy still looked grim, his features serious, belying the smiles and congratulations he had offered Richard when first official news of the engagement reached him. *He does not approve.* The thought struck Richard all at once, passing through his mind almost as quickly as it registered there. *And what do I care if he does not? My life is my own: it's no business of Darcy's who I associate with.*

This brought to mind another *associate*, one whose presence neither man had discussed in their brief reunion. The time would come, Richard supposed, for Wickham to be mentioned but he certainly would not seek to do so. How could he admit to Darcy that he not only worked with

Wickham - which circumstance was somewhat beyond his control - but that the man had become almost a friend? *Almost*, Richard reminded himself darkly. *I still do not trust him. I learnt that lesson only too well years ago. But he is useful to me...and doubtless, I am, to him.* He was not quite persuaded Wickham's assistance was entirely altruistic. There would be a cost exacted, he was certain, and when it came he must be ready to pay or risk who knew what level of destruction. Wickham might be a poor friend but he was a far worse enemy, and Richard was unwilling to unleash him on the happy life he was finally building here, with Jane Bennet at his side.

"Well!" Mr Bennet declared, slamming his empty glass down on the table with a thud. "Let us return and join the ladies. I have no doubt they are missing us!"

Richard returned Mr Bennet's chuckle with a smile but noticed that Darcy's features remained impassive. He wondered that his cousin had never mentioned knowing the Bennets, or at least never mentioned how well they seemed to be acquainted with one another. He supposed it was a given, with Netherfield Park lying so close by. He must ask what Mr and Miss Bingley had made of them, for whilst he had met Darcy's friends only once or twice he remembered them being amiable and friendly.

"Ah, Mary is playing!" Mr Bennet remarked as the trio of gentlemen made a weaving path down the corridor towards the parlour. "How quiet Longbourn has been without her here!" He winced, as she hit a wrong note. "And how in-need of a tune that old piano grows."

"She plays well," Darcy said, with a fervent loyalty that surprised Richard. He turned to look at his cousin and saw the slightest hint of a smile. "And I wager music proved a key component of the friendship she formed with Georgiana."

"Georgiana!" Lydia exclaimed, catching Darcy's last word as the door opened to admit the gentlemen into the room. "We were just talking about her. This piece was hers, so Mary said."

"What a shame you could not bring her with you!" Kitty declared, from her position lolling on a settee. She scrambled to sit up, blushing and giggling at being caught in such a repose by guests.

"You will bring her to the wedding, of course," Mrs Bennet remarked, turning to scowl at Mary, whose playing had trailed off as she listened, and who began again with fervour before any critical comment could be made in the ensuing silence.

"The wedding?" Darcy looked at Richard, momentarily thunderstruck, and even Richard could think of no comment to offer. Eager he might be to see Georgiana as well as her brother, but he certainly would not hurry to invite her to Hertfordshire when Wickham was still prowling around.

*Although,* he reasoned. *Wickham seems to have another young lady in his sights, and one for better-equipped to hold her own against his worst characteristics than Georgiana might have been.*

His mind ran on, tempting him with a version of the future when they might be able to at least consider Georgiana coming here. Wickham must be securely entangled with another, if not gone altogether. He frowned. There must be some regimental business he could concoct to send Wickham away for the duration of the wedding, and if he did as his so-called-friend had asked and helped smooth the way for a union with Elizabeth Bennet, Georgiana would be safe on two sides.

Richard's eyes strayed to the corner seat where Elizabeth sat with her newly-returned father and wondered if he dared support such a match. Darcy hovered towards them, seeming drawn to that particular corner and another thought dawned on Richard, so sharp and sudden and unhelpful that he pushed it away, turning instead to greet Jane with a smile. He would not think of Wickham tonight. That was a problem he could concern himself with tomorrow. This evening he would simply relish his good fortune, and dream of the future he might have with the beautiful Jane Bennet as his bride.

# Chapter Six

"I suppose Meryton must seem dreadfully quiet to you now, compared with London!" Elizabeth remarked as she and Mary reached the edge of the small town. She had persuaded her sister to accompany her when nobody else seemed inclined to, and found, to her surprise, that she had rather enjoyed their walk. Mary had not exactly been talkative - that had never been a trait of hers - but she answered Lizzy's questions and the two had developed a pleasant rapport while they walked.

"Oh, yes." Mary feigned a sigh. "Dreadfully! I so long to be amongst *interesting people* once more..."

Lizzy glanced at her, recognising a pitch-perfect impression of Lydia, who had complained that very morning of the dearth of *interesting people* in Meryton at present. She laughed.

"You shall have to take care not to do that in the house. I do not suppose Lydia would approve of such an accurate portrayal."

Mary beamed and became herself once more, lifting a scrap of paper from her basket and consulting the list of errands she wished to complete whilst she and her sister were in town.

"What do you think? Shall we go together? Divide and conquer?"

"We might as well do them in tandem," Lizzy said, adjusting her hat as they passed two rangy soldiers, lounging against a wall. "It is not as if either of us is in a hurry."

One of the soldiers straightened as they passed, tipping his hat to them and his companion called out to them, taking a step or two closer when they did not immediately recognise him.

"Miss Elizabeth! Miss...Mary. Good morning!"

If Mary had noticed Mr Wickham's hesitation in recalling her name she did not acknowledge it but she did fall back a little, angling herself to be behind her sister and thus, Lizzy supposed, less noticeable.

"Good morning, Mr Wickham." She smiled. "This is your first time seeing my sister since her return from London, I expect! She has but lately come back to us."

Wickham bowed and Lizzy heard Mary giggle nervously at her shoulder.

"I see you are intent on some errands this morning," he remarked, spotting their basket. "I do not suppose I could be of any assistance?"

"Are you not on duty?" Lizzy arched an eyebrow, peering past him to his colleague, who had straightened to attention and kept his gaze fixed on the middle-distance, the picture of diligence.

"Ah." Wickham's smile slipped. "Yes, you are quite right." He shrugged his broad shoulders and grinned again. "I suppose even chivalry is no excuse to shirk one's duties."

"Indeed not, Mr Wickham." Lizzy waved as he bowed again, returning to his post with evident reluctance. "Come along, Mary," she said, slipping her arm through Mary's and tugging her down the road. "Let's make a start."

"I see Mr Wickham is still a fixture," Mary remarked, almost under her breath but not quite low enough a whisper that Lizzy did not hear her.

"A fixture?" She bristled. "If you mean is he still a friend, then yes, Mary. He is a friend to our whole family, so you needn't slide back into judgment just because I pause to pass the time of day with someone who is known to us all."

Mary bit her lip and Elizabeth instantly regretted her outburst. Why was she so adamant about defending Mr Wickham to her sister? Mary's question might have been entirely innocent. In the time since she had been home, there had been scarcely a mention of Mr Wickham. What was she to think but that his friendship might have slipped in comparison to Colonel Fitzwilliam, who had fast become a regular visitor to Longbourn.

"We are not such close friends," Lizzy said, after a moment, wishing she could make her voice sound normal. Trembling the way it did made it sound as if she cared far more for Mr Wickham than was truthful. "But he was kind enough to stop and speak to us. It would have been rude not to acknowledge him. Look, here is the glovemakers. Do you have Mama's note?"

Mary reached back into her basket, retrieving the specifications Mama had dictated to them and passed a scrap of paper to Elizabeth, who bounded into the shop, grateful for a task and equally grateful to escape what felt like scrutiny from her silent sister.

While the shopkeeper retreated to his store cupboard in search of Elizabeth's order, she feigned interest in his display of newer items before allowing her gaze to travel, quite naturally, to the window. Mary stood patiently outside, waiting for her return. Her features were neutral, not clouded with concern, as Lizzy had half-expected to see them. Perhaps she had imagined the censure in Mary's voice about Mr Wickham. *Your imagination is playing tricks on you. What does Mary care about who you are friends with?* And what did it matter to Elizabeth what Mary thought about her, anyway? She had rarely cared to court her sister's good opinion before her trip to London. Had things changed so much in a few weeks?

Mary startled and Elizabeth startled with her. Something had caught Mary's attention, for now she turned away from the window, waving into the distance. Not something. *Someone.* Lizzy took a step to the side, wishing the small window was larger, so she might see whether Mary had now fallen victim, herself, to George Wickham's warm greetings and handsome smiles.

"Here we are, Miss Bennet." The shopkeeper emerged from behind a door, clutching the parcel she had come to collect, and she smiled and thanked him, taking it and hurrying out of the door in eagerness to see whether Mr Wickham's manner with Mary was quite as friendly as it was with her. He was handsome and charming, but she dared to think he had shown particular pleasantness to her and she was a little reluctant to be proved mistaken.

"Have you decided to abandon your work altogether, then, Mr -" Lizzy had begun speaking whilst still in the building but her words faltered when she looked up and realised, with surprise, that it was not Mr Wickham that had hailed Mary at all. "Mr Darcy," she finished, faintly. "Good morning."

"Good morning." He tipped his hat to her, stepping back to allow her ample space to step out of the shop and into the street. "Your sister tells me you are running errands today." He glanced past Elizabeth and into the shop. "I trust you are making progress."

"Progress?" Elizabeth realised she still clutched Mrs Bennet's new gloves and with a faint smile she leaned over to drop them unceremoniously into Mary's empty basket. "Yes. We are making progress."

Mary was looking at her expectantly, clearing her throat pointedly when Elizabeth did not immediately pepper Mr Darcy with questions.

"And you? What brings you to Meryton?"

"Errands." Darcy's smile was not quite so wide nor as charming as Mr Wickham's, but it did improve him greatly. He was very handsome, particularly when he did not scowl as he had done when first he came to Hertfordshire. Lizzy was staring, and all at once she nodded, turning back to the street and tugging Mary along with her.

"Well, you must not allow us to detain you from your tasks."

"Very well," Darcy replied, his voice ringing with what might have been disappointment. "Good day to you both."

"We might have walked with him a step," Mary whispered when they were far enough away that she was in no danger of being overheard. "I dare say our paths will cross again, and our errands take us to many of the same places. He could have accompanied us -"

"He did not offer!" Elizabeth said, sharply, wondering why it stung her that he had not when Mr Wickham had been only too eager to be of service.

DARCY WATCHED ELIZABETH and Mary walk away, swallowing a bitter sense of disappointment that their interaction had been so brief. *Go after them*, a voice in his head urged him. *Ask them...*

Ask them what? He could hardly launch into a detailed discussion of the engagement between his cousin and their sister, not even if that was the very thing he longed to do. He had hoped, upon coming back to Hertfordshire, that he might be able to win Elizabeth to his side, gain her help and support in discovering what was going on between his cousin and Jane Bennet.

*Do I need help in knowing that?* He sighed. It was painfully obvious to anyone who witnessed more than a moment's interaction between the pair that they were hopelessly, irrevocably in love. At least, Richard was. Darcy knew his cousin well enough to see that his feelings were genuine. It might have been heartening, to see the ordinarily brash and self-reliant Colonel Fitzwilliam so enamoured. Indeed, Georgiana had rejoiced at the news, spinning some fantastical future where Colonel Fitzwilliam and his new bride might be persuaded to settle close to Pemberley, and waxing lyrical that it was about time Richard built for himself the home his own family had always denied him.

*But what of Charles?* Darcy regretted his role in all of this. If he had not supported Caroline - intentionally or otherwise - in her scheme to spirit Charles away to London in hopes he would forget his blossoming affection for Jane Bennet, then perhaps he would be the one whose sights were fixed on marriage. Netherfield would be a home for the prospective couple, and Richard's heart and future would be entirely altered. *And safe from harm.* This was the crux of Darcy's problem, then. It was why he had not yet written to Charles, despite his having been in Hertfordshire several days and knowing that his friend would be eagerly awaiting his note. *How can I tell him that all his suspicions are true? That she is happy with another...with my cousin?*

Darcy began to walk again, thinking with gratitude of the one letter he had been able to write and send with a clear conscience. He had told Georgiana in no uncertain terms that Richard was a changed man: soon to married and brimming over with happiness. He had the letter still about his person, for he had wanted to include some treat with it. A pretty new hair-ribbon, perhaps, or a notion that might perk up a bonnet. He wished Georgiana might be with him now, and Mrs Bennet's questions only fuelled his own. How would he ever manage to keep her from coming once the date of the wedding was fixed?

*Perhaps I do not need to*, he mused. Richard was in charge of the regiment still. If Wickham could be got rid of then Georgiana's visit might be able to take place safely in his absence.

He picked up his pace, thinking that he would call at the barracks right then and see if he could persuade his cousin to take a short break from his work. He had scarcely seen him alone, and whilst he did not seem to mind being in company with the Bennets as much as he had done once, he rather missed the freedom of being able to speak and act just as he pleased with only Richard for company.

As he reached the barracks he slowed, spotting two soldiers on duty at the front of the building. One he did not know but the other he recognised almost immediately, his lips turning down in a scowl. *Speak of the devil and behold he will appear!* he thought, grimly, even though he had not spoken of Wickham at all. *The fellow seems to be conjured even by my thoughts of late.* He straightened his flawless cravat and continued along his path, determined that the presence of his old foe would not deter him from calling on his cousin. The arrival of a third soldier halted his progress, though, and when he recognised Richard, he drew to a halt, his lips quirking at the thought he might witness Wickham's public dressing-down.

He could not hear the conversation and he almost leaned closer, as if that might render the trio not too distant to be overheard. Wickham did not seem dismayed, nor Richard particularly critical. He smiled! Yes, his cousin, Colonel Richard Fitzwilliam, was smiling and talking with George Wickham as if the two were not enemies but colleagues. *Friends*!

Darcy's blood ran cold in his veins. This was betrayal, pure and simple. Worse, even, than the original act of Wickham attempting to seduce Georgiana. He had been acting as he always did - for profit or pleasure or his own merry wishes.

Richard had known that - had witnessed it all, and the aftermath as Georgiana recovered. How could he now bear to associate with Wickham at all, let alone smile and laugh with the fellow as if none of the past had happened?

He remained pinned in place for a moment, waiting, hoping, he might see some change come over his cousin. *It is an act, surely. Politeness for the sake of their witness.* But the third soldier retreated, sent on some errand or to accomplish some task and Richard did not immediately turn on Wickham. Nothing changed in his manner at all. Wickham's laugh carried on the morning breeze to Darcy's ears and he could bear no more. He turned on his heel and stalked away, snatching his letter to Georgiana and tearing it to shreds as he walked, letting the scraps of paper fall where they may. He would not send this letter: he would not dare. *How can I risk bringing Georgiana here, when even her cousin has forgiven George Wickham his misdeeds and will stand by and allow him to commit them all over again?*

His breath came sharply as he walked, from agitation rather than exertion, and he had rounded a corner before he relaxed, safe in the knowledge he would not be seen. Yanking his hat off his head, he massaged away the beginnings of a crippling headache and wondered when he had become so estranged from the cousin he had always thought of as a friend.

*What loyalty do I owe him now? He clearly bears me none.*

A tiny spark of conscience urged him back, suggested that he did not know for certain what he had witnessed, and surely there would be an explanation if only Richard could be offered the chance to give it.

*I have heard explanations enough from Wickham concerning his misdeeds*, he thought, grimly. *I do not need to hear my cousin come to his defence. No, Richard Fitzwilliam may be my cousin, but he is no longer my friend. And that being the case, I need no longer feel torn in my support of Charles Bingley.* He would write to Charles, then, and tell him all that had transpired. Richard and Jane might be engaged, but they were not yet married. And did Charles not deserve as much of a chance at happiness as Richard? *I owe him that much, when I am the one that helped cause the separation to begin with.*

# Chapter Seven

Richard waited a full minute after George Wickham walked away before he let his smile drop, once he was certain his so-called friend would not look back.

*So-called friend.* How had Wickham become anything close to a friend, so-called or otherwise? Richard could not believe how he had allowed himself to once again be manipulated by George Wickham, or how much harder it would be to extricate himself from the man's grip now that Darcy was back in Hertfordshire.

This short conversation with Wickham had made one thing abundantly clear to Richard, and that was that whatever influence he thought he had over Wickham it did not extend as far as he had imagined. He had tried everything short of actively bribing Wickham to leave Meryton, and he had only held off from doing that because he knew it would betray just how eagerly Richard wanted him gone. Knowledge was, and had always been, power to George Wickham and Richard was certainly not about to give him any more of that.

He sighed, rubbing at the frown that had carved itself into his forehead and wondering if he could somehow persuade Colonel Forster to write and request Wickham's presence at his side. That might succeed in making him go, but how could he pose the question to Forster without garnering further questioning from him, or, worse, risk him sharing the truth over too much brandy that Wickham's summons had originated with Colonel Fitzwilliam oh-so-coincidentally at the time of his wedding.

*There is time yet,* he reminded himself. He was sure he would conceive of a fool-proof plan to banish George Wickham before the wedding was upon them and before Georgiana stepped foot into Hertfordshire. *And before Darcy can learn that we have been like friends during my tenure in Meryton.* This was the secret he most wanted to keep to himself, for he knew his cousin would not view any association with George Wickham as wise, no matter what line of defence Richard mounted. He was not entirely sure he had convinced himself, pragmatic or not, that what he was doing was right. *Is it worth all this to keep Wickham in check?* he wondered. Maybe he should beat him to the punch and confess all to Darcy, let the chips fall where they may. He grew serious. No. He was not ready to sacrifice the one friendship that truly valued.

"Colonel Fitzwilliam!"

Richard straightened at the sound of someone calling him by name - a female someone. He turned, managing to rearrange his features into a smile just in time to spot Elizabeth Bennet and her sister walking across the busy square towards him.

"Good morning!"

"Good morning, Miss Elizabeth." He bowed, recalling the name of the quiet, dark-haired sister as he straightened and deploying it immediately. "And Miss Mary. Good day." He made a show of peering into their basket and chuckled. "I trust your morning has been successful?"

"Moderately," Elizabeth said, shouldering her paper-wrapped burdens and nudging Mary as she did so. "We are about to make our way home to Longbourn but could not resist passing by the barracks to say hello to our friends."

"Alas, you have found only me!" Colonel Fitzwilliam assumed a tragical position, and both girls laughed.

"Did your cousin find you?" Mary asked, sliding her basket from one arm to another.

"Darcy? Is he here?" Concern flashed through Richard's veins and he glanced around as if expecting at that moment to see his cousin lurking in some shadowy enclave, poised to pounce. *Nonsense*, he reminded himself. *Your guilty conscience is working overtime.*

"We saw him a little while ago," Elizabeth said, with a vague, fixed smile. "I suppose he was too busy."

"He mentioned he wished to see you." Mary shot her sister a look Richard could not quite read. "Perhaps he has been waylaid."

"Well, he shall know precisely where to find me," Richard said, with a philosophical shrug. "I am duty-bound to stay here all day." Chivalry reproached him and he reached forward to take Mary's basket. "Which is not to say I can be of no assistance to you ladies. You would benefit from an escort back to Longbourn, I am sure. Fear not, I'm sure I can find a recruit or two with time on their hands that would be more than content to carry your purchases for you."

"Oh, that's not necessary!" Mary said, with a shy smile.

"But very kind of you to offer." Elizabeth returned her sister's glare with one of her own. "Jane is at home," she put in, with a knowing look. "But I am sure she will be pleased to hear that we ran into you."

"You must tell her I was hard at work," Richard said, with a grin. "So busy and productive that I could not spare more than a moment, but when I did I enquired chiefly after her wellbeing." He raised his eyebrows. "And is she well?"

"Perfectly!" Elizabeth sighed. "Is she ever anything else?"

"You are goading me into saying something I may regret, Miss Elizabeth." Richard's smile grew. "If I agree with you that Jane is *perfectly well, always*, I am undoubtedly committing some unforeseen slight against the two charming young ladies before me. If I favour you, it is a slight you will hurry home to report to Jane, and I shall be forced to pay for my sins when next we meet." He made a show of sealing his lips. "Therefore I will stay silent and merely wish you good day."

Elizabeth laughed, sliding her free arm through Mary's and steering her back towards the road.

"Good day, Colonel Fitzwilliam! No doubt we shall see you again soon. Perhaps this evening?"

"Perhaps," Richard said, waving at them. He paused, rethinking his commitments for the day and deciding, on a whim, that he would be better served by seeing Darcy than Jane that evening, whatever his heart might dictate. "I must confess I think it altogether likely you will not see me before tomorrow, and you must send my apologies to your family."

He straightened to attention and bowed them goodbye before turning back towards the barracks. He would write a note to Darcy now, inviting him to join him in dining at the inn favoured by members of the militia and thinking that to be with his cousin in the presence of so many other loud, amiable fellows might be to put him more at his ease.

*Besides, it is the one place in all Meryton I can guarantee Wickham will not be this evening. I have just ensured he will be assigned elsewhere...*

If he must discuss Wickham with Darcy, better he do so in public. With witnesses. His jaw set uncomfortably. He did not relish the thought of the evening ahead of him, but he must address the George-Wickham-shaped elephant in the room sooner rather than later, and until he did so he would not be able to fully relax, nor fully enjoy spending time with his cousin. Better to face the music now than risk discovery later.

*And if I plan for it this evening, I shall have all afternoon to strategize my best plan of success.*

THE SPRING SUNSHINE peeped through the window of Jane's bedroom as she sorted through her wardrobe. She generally kept her clothes well-maintained, having been reminded often how her dresses would pass from her to her sisters and must be neat enough to be worn sometimes by two or three subsequent wearers before being consigned to the rag bag. She was careful by nature, though, and took pride in maintaining and making-over her dresses, seeing them rendered new and fashionable again with the smallest degree of attention.

That morning, she laid down the last of her dresses and turned her attention to a pile of ribbon and lace she sorted through, searching for just the right details to revivify an old bonnet.

"Jaaaannneee."

Lydia's shrill cry was audible long before she threw open the door to Jane's room without knocking and waltzed in, collapsing so suddenly and abruptly on the bed that Jane hardly had time to leap to her feet before being crushed.

"Oh dear, whatever is the matter!" she asked, with a merry laugh that soon dissolved into silence when Lydia groaned into the pile of dresses she was now wrinkling into oblivion. "Please don't destroy my entire wardrobe, Lydia. They shall be yours someday."

This was enough to bring Lydia to her senses, at least enough to rise to a seat and scowl down at the clothes as if their mere existence were an offence to her.

"I never get anything new!" she said, her lower lip jutting out in dissatisfaction. "You cannot imagine how it feels to always be dressed in other people's clothes!"

"Nonsense!" Jane said, reaching down to rescue her dresses and hanging them carefully on a hook out of harm's way. "The dress you are wearing now was made up special just for you."

"Last year!" Lydia sniffed, plucking at the puffed sleeves that had been her whole heart's desire when she had insisted upon them, but which had lately fallen a little out of fashion and were borne with undisguised disappointment by the youngest and most stylish - in her own opinion, at least – of the Bennet sisters.

"Here." Jane delved into her scrap bag, emerging with a pretty length of lace. She passed it to Lydia with a smile. "This is the very thing to freshen it up for spring, don't you think?"

"I suppose." Lydia let out a long sigh but was quick to snatch the lace out of Jane's hands before she could second-guess her generosity.

"I suppose you shall buy all new things for your trousseau," Lydia ventured, darting a sly look towards Jane's dresses. "None of these will be suitable when you are mistress of your own estate."

"Why ever not?" Jane laughed, running an affectionate palm across the brocade of one dress, a favourite, which had won her more than one devout admirer after being worn to an assembly for the first time.

"Do you love Colonel Fitzwilliam?" Lydia asked, changing tack and catching Jane by surprise by the bluntness of her question.

"Of course." She turned back to her dresses, strangely eager to hide her face from Lydia's eyes, certain that she might somehow see more than Jane meant her to in the shadows that danced across her features. "I should hardly have agreed to marry him if I did not."

"But you loved Mr Bingley."

Jane froze, turning at last to glance at Lydia and surprised by the genuine curiosity in her sister's eyes. Lydia was not teasing her, nor nosing around for crumbs of gossip. She frowned, rubbing her nose thoughtfully.

"Didn't you?"

With a low sigh, Jane freed her hands and sat back on the bed beside her sister, reaching for the lace that Lydia was twisting in her fingers and smoothing it out, before folding it neatly into a square.

"I thought I did," she confessed. "Or rather, I thought he loved me." She smiled, sadly. "I was perhaps a little too quick to trust my heart instead of my brain."

Lydia shook her head fiercely.

"One has nothing to do with the other! Love is something one feels, something one is consumed by. It can't be dictated to by logic or law."

"Law?" Jane arched an eyebrow and Lydia shrugged her shoulders, giggling.

"You know what I mean. I think people - and by people, I mean Lizzy and Mary, let us be clear - put far too much stock in doing what is right and proper, especially where love is concerned."

"You would prefer nobody think about anything at all but do precisely as they please?"

"Of course!" Lydia threw herself back on the bed again, staring up at the ceiling with a dreamy sigh. "I have said as much to Denny. If he should like to get married I should happily run away with him." She turned a wicked smile towards Jane. "Do you think we would make it as far as Scotland before Papa discovered us?"

"I think you oughtn't to joke about things like that," Jane said, primly. She knew Lydia was only teasing her but there was something so scandalous about the very idea of her youngest sister running away with anyone - however unlikely - that she did not like to tempt fate by talking about it. "And if Mr Denny has any sense he will not mention it again."

"He is avoiding me," Lydia laughed. "I think he was rather traumatised by the suggestion of our running away. He is quite convinced Papa doesn't like him."

"I don't think Papa does!"

"That's because Papa has eyes for nobody by Colonel Fitzwilliam." She pinched Jane's knee. "I think it's jolly lucky you like Colonel Fitzwilliam even a little because Papa wants him for a son-in-law and he would demand one of us marry him if you didn't."

"I think you are speaking nonsense, Lydia, and if you have come here only to plague me, I shall bid you adieu and go back to my work." Jane stood, returning her attention to her dresses for a long, quiet moment before Lydia spoke again. This time her voice was soft and serious and bade Jane turn back and give her her full attention.

"But you do like Colonel Fitzwilliam, don't you? You love him?"

"I both like him and care for him very much," Jane said, skirting carefully past *love*, which she was certain Lydia would notice and comment on. *I cannot say for certain whether I love him or not!* she confided to herself, biting her lip to keep from saying it aloud. *I have no idea what it means to love anyone at all, or I should not have lost my heart so swiftly and completely to Mr Bingley.* She bit down harder until she felt tears prick at the corners of her eyes. *And I should not care that he has abandoned me absolutely.*

"What if Mr Bingley came back?"

Lydia's question seemed to turn so swiftly in the very direction that Jane's thoughts had run that she was not sure, at first, that she had not spoken them aloud. It took her a full minute to formulate a reply.

"I doubt very much that he will." She smiled, surprised at the effort it cost her. "And even if he did, I have made my decision. I am happy with my choice, Lydia. Colonel Fitzwilliam is a good man and a kind one, and he cares for me very much. We shall make our life together and it will be a very happy one."

Lydia rolled over, the action muffling a loud groan.

"You do realise this means we shall forever be linked to Mr Darcy! He will be your cousin, Jane!"

"In-law," Jane clarified, her lips quirking into a smile. "And is he really so terrible?"

"Elizabeth will not be happy!" Lydia declared, wriggling herself upright and bolting towards the door, a mischievous smile on her face. "Which makes me rather more accepting of the idea."

She pulled the door closed behind her with a bang, thundering away to torment another of her sister and Jane's expression softened as she stared after her, pondering a secret she fancied she knew. Elizabeth rendered unhappy by a permanent and ongoing connection with Mr Darcy? *I am not entirely sure I agree with that.*

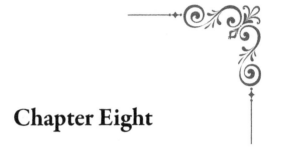

# Chapter Eight

Darkness had descended over Meryton by the time Fitzwilliam Darcy arrived at the inn specified by his cousin. His pride rankled a little at being summoned by letter, and he had been tempted to send a refusal by return, merely to put off having to see Richard that evening. He had been unable to think of a suitable cause, though. Richard knew he was alone at Netherfield, and he further knew that any work Darcy undertook while absent from both London and Pemberley could be delayed by an hour or two. Furthermore, his curiosity gnawed away at him, rendering him useless for most of the day. How could he hope to proceed without being driven mad if he did not take this opportunity to question his cousin about what he had seen - or thought he had seen - that morning in Meryton?

*Explain to me how you can stand around and talk to Wickham as if he were a friend and not a sworn enemy to us both. Explain how you have not warned Mr Bennet, Jane, Elizabeth - Elizabeth! - of the risk they take in pursuing a friendship with him.*

In truth, this caused him as much if not more pain than all the rest. Darcy well recalled the annoyance with which his warning of caution regarding George Wickham had been received by Elizabeth Bennet. She judged him for warning her at all and had Richard said even a word in tune since then, with or without Darcy there to witness it, it would have gone a good way in repairing things between them.

*This is not about Elizabeth*, he reminded himself, although he was forced to swallow the feeling that almost everything he did of late was about Elizabeth in some shape or form. Taking one last, fortifying breath he pushed open the door to the noisy, crowded inn and stepped inside, shedding his coat and hat and scanning the interior for the familiar shape of his cousin. At last, he spied Richard, sitting at a table in a quieter corner of the inn, nursing a glass of ale and perusing a stack of papers. He looked up as he sensed Darcy approach.

"You came!"

"You asked me to." Darcy could hear the gruffness in his voice as he sat down, but Richard did not seem to notice it. He happily folded his stack of papers into a leather case and slid it onto an empty chair between them.

"I hear you were in Meryton earlier today!" Richard smiled, oblivious to the scowl Darcy could feel settling over his features. "What a shame you could not spare a quarter-hour to call at the barracks."

Darcy stared at him in disbelief. Did he have no idea that Darcy had, indeed, spared a quarter-hour and walked to the barracks with a mind to call on his cousin? Did he even consider what Darcy had witnessed that prevented him from going ahead with it?

"It matters not," Richard continued, his smile dimming slightly in the face of Darcy's scowl. "For we can dine together now. I trust you do not mind this place? It hardly compares with Netherfield, I dare say, even when you dine alone. But I have come here often since my tenure at Meryton began and I have to say I have grown to like the place." He waved over the proprietor and placed an order for them both. Darcy still had not spoken a word beyond his first greeting.

"I have been drowning in reports all day!" Richard confessed. "I swear, I almost miss fighting at the front. At least then one could be a man of action and when was not, one could be at liberty to rest. In my position at the barracks, there is always writing to be done or reports to be read." He pulled a face. "And we both recall how I excelled in my schooling as a boy."

Darcy said nothing, thinking over his own afternoon. He had stewed for much of it, driven to distraction as he thought over Richard's apparent friendship with Wickham and striven to put a positive - and then not so positive - slant on it. At last, he had sat at his desk and penned a letter he had put off writing, scrawling out a hasty note to Charles that he had dispatched to London almost before the ink had dried. He had not written to Georgiana, and now, faced with Richard, he rather regretted doing either.

"Come, Darcy! It is not such a hardship to spare me an hour and eat together, is it?" Richard laughed, but the sound grew desperate when it received nothing but a stony glare in response. "You have scarcely said a word." His cousin's features fell. "You are not unwell, I hope?"

"Not unwell, no." Darcy leaned his elbows on the table, folding one hand into the other, and resting his chin on them both to fix his cousin with a level stare. "A little confused..."

"Confused?" Richard grinned, sensing the beginning of a joke. "Well, share your thoughts, and let us see if between us we might puzzle out a solution!"

"I came to the barracks earlier."

Richard had lifted his glass to his drink and was partway through taking a sip as Darcy said this. The liquid caught in his throat as he swallowed and he coughed once or twice to get it down.

"You did? I was not told."

"I did not call." Darcy could hear the bitter note in his voice and wished he could rid himself of the anger he felt towards his cousin. There would be an explanation, surely? There must be. Of all people, Darcy knew he could trust the man opposite him. *At least, I thought I could.*

"I saw you speaking with George Wickham."

The delivery had been flat, devoid of all emotion, yet still it seemed to weigh heavily in the air between the two cousins.

"Ah." Richard said at last. He reached for his glass again, taking a hasty sip. "You saw me speaking with Wickham." He paused. "Well, you know, Darcy, we have been forced to speak to one another from time to time. It is not my choice, I confess, but he is my subordinate officer, and -"

"You seemed more like friends than colleagues." Darcy shrugged his shoulders. "I suppose it is easy to forget what the man did when you are not forced to see the impact he had on Georgiana day after day." His voice dropped. "When you have not lived half your life being plagued by him."

Richard's face paled but he said nothing.

"Wickham is not to be trusted," Darcy said. "I thought we were on the same page about that."

"Wickham is not to be trusted," Richard repeated, slowly nodding in agreement. His expression soured. "Are you suggesting that I am also not to be trusted?"

Darcy said nothing, unsure how to formulate a reply that would not catch the angry glint in his cousin's eyes and escalate it. Silence seemed entirely adequate to the task though and Richard let out a bark of bitter laughter, leaning back in his chair.

"I see. You have decided that because I was forced to speak to the man - forced by my job, mind you, and forced to do so on your behalf, I might add - that I am part of some great scheme against you." Richard shook his head. "I know we have not been in close contact of late, Darcy, but did I not do everything in my power to help you resolve matters with Georgiana? Have we not always been friends as well as cousins? But you have made your mind up about me after witnessing a conversation - part of a conversation - and are not even willing to let me explain myself."

"What explanation can you give? You associate freely with George Wickham. You have dined with him at Longbourn." Here Darcy could feel pain flash across his face and strove to remain neutral. "Your presence together has vouchsafed for him to be welcomed there as a friend when we both know he is not to be trusted."

"Do you think I am to be trusted, Darcy?" Richard's voice had grown low and bitter, tinged with hurt. "You have not properly congratulated me upon my engagement to Jane. You seem surprised that it has happened at all. I dare say you think she marries below her status in choosing me. Or perhaps I am daring to make my own decisions without consulting you, the great Fitzwilliam Darcy, on every detail of my choice. You consider yourself an authority on everything but when have you ever had to struggle for anything in your life?"

Richard pushed his chair back from the table and stood, stopping to grasp his case of reports.

"I think I shall dine at the barracks this evening. Enjoy your meal." He did not wait for Darcy to make any kind of reply but stalked from the inn without a backward glance.

RICHARD'S ANGER HAD barely dissipated by the time he had marched back across the threshold of his private study in the bowels of the barracks. He threw his case down onto his desk with more force than he meant to, sending the pile of reports it contained skittering in all directions. Cursing, he bent to retrieve them, piling them all back together higgledy-piggledy before stalking over to his drinks cabinet and pouring himself a measure of brandy.

*How dare Darcy...how dare he!*

He took a sip of his drink, allowing his eyes to slowly come back into focus on the room around him. His stomach turned over as he thought back over their argument. It had not been like speaking to Darcy at all. It had been like...like speaking to his brother. He kicked at a cabinet but instead of giving any vent to his feelings all it did was send pain shooting up his leg and he staggered back to his desk, sinking heavily into his chair and beginning to sort his reports back into a chronological pile. The slow, methodical work calmed him and by the time it was done he was rational again. Rational, and irritated.

*This is not Darcy's fault*, he reasoned. *It is mine. No, it is Wickham's.* If there was one man in all of England upon whose shoulders blame for Richard's current predicament could be placed it was George Wickham's. He had been the one to trifle with Georgiana's affections, after all. *And whose fault was it that he even met Georgiana?*

With a scowl and a sigh, Richard pushed his work aside and turned back to his brandy. He had spent the better part of a year trying to swallow the truth that would not be swallowed. George Wickham might have set his sights on Georgiana with nefarious intent, but if Richard had not been the one to make introductions - or, as the case turned out to be, to renew their acquaintance - would things ever have progressed as far or as quickly as they had done?

*If I had confessed the truth sooner, perhaps Darcy and I would be on better footing now.* This was supposition only, but Richard had no cause to doubt it. He knew he was prone to seeing prejudice from Darcy where there was none because he felt a pre-emptive degree of guilt whenever mention was made of either Wickham or Georgiana for the role he had played in their disastrous courtship.

Yet Georgiana did not seem to bear any kind of grudge against him. As soon as she had been safely returned to Pemberley and George Wickham went to ground, Richard had retreated across the ocean, seeking to work out his anger and anxiety on the battlefield and it had worked for a time. Georgiana had written to him, at last, pleading with him to come home, and at last, when leave was granted and his service required in England he had come home, but he had not yet reconnected with Georgiana. He was not quite sure he dared to. Would she be the same Georgiana she had been in Ramsgate? Before Ramsgate? Before Wickham? Or would she be changed, as Darcy was changed?

He had not acknowledged as much about his cousin, for Darcy had always been aloof, but since Georgiana, he had bordered on antisocial with anyone except those he knew well.

Now, Richard feared, even old friends - family members - were at risk of permanent estrangement.

*Deservedly.* Richard clenched his hands around his glass, draining its contents and refiling it with a second drink almost without being aware of doing so.

He would make it up with Darcy in the morning, he told himself, leaning back in his chair and rolling his face towards the ceiling. They had fallen out before and made amends. They would do so this time.

*And I will tell him the truth*, Richard thought. *I will explain it all.* That he, too, had been deceived into trusting George Wickham once and been blackmailed into trusting him again. He knew better, and from now on he would do better.

With a sigh, he placed his glass down carefully, sliding it just out of reach, lest he drink too much, too quickly, and turned his attention back to his work. If he no longer had the excuse of spending time with his cousin there was no reason to waste the evening in rumination. Better to work and have something to show for his hours of isolation.

Ignoring the grumble in the pit of his stomach, he threw himself into his work and barely noticed the hours ticking by as evening slid into night.

# Chapter Nine

Whilst Elizabeth often preferred the company of her sisters, even she could not object to a solitary walk in the countryside surrounding Longbourn. She could dictate her own pace, let her thoughts travel wherever they wanted and had to humour nobody but herself. Her mood soared as she scrambled over a stile and into a neighbouring field, landing firmly in a muddy puddle and thinking, with regret, of the state of her hem.

*It is hardly the first time I have returned home in a dress thick with mud!* she thought, with a rueful smile. She recalled the time Jane was taken ill at Netherfield, when she had marched the whole three miles there, barely noticing the state of the weather, and arrived dishevelled, drenched and mud-soaked. *What an arrival that was, and what an impression it made on Netherfield's inhabitants!* She glanced up at the horizon, surprised to spot a figure approaching her and even more surprised to recognise it as belonging to just such a one of those *Netherfield inhabitants* that had just crossed her mind.

Mr Darcy had not noticed her yet. His gaze was fixed on the ground before him, his features drawn down into a scowl that made Elizabeth's own smile fade. How quickly she had grown used to *Mr Darcy without a scowl* that seeing him with one again rather jolted her. She recalled his attempt at friendliness in Meryton the previous day and regretted that she had not been more amenable to it. Of course he was not as friendly as he might have been, but compared to how he had appeared upon their very first meeting he was kindness itself and she had snubbed, rather than encouraged, him. Taking a deep breath, she decided that his appearance now was an opportunity given to her by Providence to make up the difference, and she determined she would be the first to make an effort.

"Mr Darcy!" She waved to him, forcing her lips into a smile as the two walkers drew closer to one another. "Good morning!"

"Elizabeth, I -" He came a sudden halt, surprised to see her and still half-lost in his thoughts. It took a moment before he could return her smile with anything approaching the same but at last he managed it, doffing his hat for good measure. "Good morning." He glanced around them as if surprised that his route march had led him so far afield.

They stared at each other in silence for a moment, neither one sure how to proceed. At last it was Darcy who spoke first.

"I see you made it safely home from Meryton. I trust you and Miss Mary accomplished all of your tasks yesterday."

This nebulous statement was so surprising that Elizabeth laughed, which seemed to break the tension between them. Even Mr Darcy smiled, she saw, and was thus encouraged to answer in a more friendly manner than she might have done had they met an hour or two sooner.

"Yes, thank you. And it occurs to me that I was a little short when we met. Forgive me."

Darcy shrugged his shoulders as if to indicate he had not noticed any slight, nor held it against her. Silence fell once again and this time Elizabeth was the one to break it.

"Are you walking for pleasure or with a destination in mind?"

"Neither." Darcy's grimace softened. "And you?"

"Neither." Elizabeth risked a smile. "Perhaps, in that case, we might walk a little way together? Unless you prefer to be left alone." Her eyes fluttered closed. What had possessed her to make such a suggestion? Had she not, mere moments earlier, been rejoicing in blessed solitude? Why now seek companionship - and that of Mr Darcy, of all people! She opened her mouth to rescind the suggestion, poised to turn and hurry off in another direction, but he spoke before she was able to do either.

"I think that would be a fine suggestion, Miss Elizabeth." He dipped his head. "I shall allow you to determine our route, for if I recall correctly you are far better acquainted with these lands than I am."

Elizabeth continued the path she had been taking, which would lead eventually back towards Netherfield. It had not been her goal, but now she wondered if perhaps some part deep inside her had not intended this all along. They walked in silence for a few moments, making occasional comments about the weather, the abundance of greenery, the flourish of spring after a long, unendurable winter.

"Did you see your cousin?" Elizabeth asked, when there was a break in their conversation. "Mary and I happened across Colonel Fitzwilliam on our way home yesterday and he said that you had not made it to the barracks. I hope you did manage to see him, after all."

"Yes."

Darcy's voice was terse, so quiet that Elizabeth immediately glanced his way. His scowl was firmly in place again, looking fiercer and more ferocious than ever.

"I trust he is well," she ventured, curious at the sudden change that had come over her companion.

"He is," Darcy said, sharply. After a moment in which he seemed to be at war with himself, he stopped walking altogether and turned towards her. "In truth, Elizabeth, it is on account of my cousin that I have been out walking this morning. I have been trying to make sense of a situation I cannot begin to understand and - and to work out a little of my frustrations by walking."

"Ah. And how do you fare, in either case?"

"Not well!" Darcy admitted, with a self-deprecating laugh. They began to walk once more and Elizabeth weighed her words carefully before speaking again.

"You know, I have it on good authority - not my own, for I am a great one for stewing on my problems and building them up into great catastrophes in the privacy of my own mind - but others tell me that it can, on occasion, help to talk about one's concerns."

Darcy did not reply straight away but a glance in his general direction confirmed that he had heard her. She held her peace, trusting that the presence of a silent audience might do what no degree of inquiry would. After a moment or two she was proved right, as Darcy took a long breath in and began.

"I did meet with my cousin yesterday, although not at the time I planned. We met for dinner and I - I went there angry with something I believed I knew." He removed his hat, raking a hand through his dark hair before replacing it firmly atop his head. "You know my feelings about George Wickham -" He held a hand up, looking at her with such anguish in his dark eyes that Lizzy was stunned into silence and could not have given any response, even if she had wanted to. "I know you are inclined towards him but please, Lizzy, trust that my animosity towards George Wickham is not without cause. Richard, too, bore the same grudge." His voice dropped to a grim whisper. "At least, I thought he did. It seems I was mistaken, for the two are friends, or act as if they were. I rather railed at Richard for fostering such an association, for appearing to forgive Wickham for - for what he did." He had stopped himself mid-sentence, turning away from any actual allusion to what had occurred and Lizzy's curiosity burned within her. She had dismissed Darcy's warnings about George Wickham as simply a display of his pride, yet another example of him considering himself better than his neighbours. Now she wondered if she had been mistaken. Perhaps there was more to it than she had ever imagined. This was not the time to talk about George Wickham, though and so, reluctantly, she swallowed her questions and tried a different tack.

"I do not believe Colonel Fitzwilliam to be distrustful," she ventured. "He has been nothing but kind to my family. And of course, Jane cares so deeply for him."

"She does?" Darcy looked stricken, his face paling. "She cares for him more than she did for Bingley, do you suppose?"

Lizzy was torn. On the one hand, she wished to keep her sister's counsel. What business was it of Fitzwilliam Darcy where her heart lay? Yet he looked so unsettled that it was all she could do not to leap to offer a response. In the end, she found a middle ground, nodding fervently but offering no further commentary.

"Then Richard is fortunate, indeed," Darcy said, his frown sinking still more heavily onto his features. He seemed to notice suddenly that their walk took them closer to Netherfield, and he turned them around, pledging to do the chivalrous duty of escorting Elizabeth safely home, as he ought, and making a great effort to turn their conversation back to simpler, happier things.

"YOU CANNOT MEAN TO suggest that Henry Fielding is a better author than Samuel Richardson!" Elizabeth exclaimed as she and Mr Darcy drew within sight of Longbourn.

"Correct. I do not suggest it. I declare it a fact."

Darcy could not quite keep his lips from quirking into a smile and betrayed himself entirely by laughing at the look of exasperation Elizabeth shot him.

"And here, Miss Elizabeth, it seems we have made it back to Longbourn in one piece." He was poised to take his leave when Elizabeth laid a light hand on his arm to detain him.

"You will come indoors, won't you? I'm sure Papa will be pleased to see you again, and Mama and Jane..." She trailed off, evidently sensing his reluctance, and dealt one last trump card. "And Mary! You cannot mean to have walked all this way without checking on Mary. I have it on good authority she received a letter from Georgiana just yesterday..." Her voice took on a teasing, wheedling tone and Darcy made a great show of resigning himself to his fate.

Privately, he was delighted to be so eagerly encouraged to stay, and his breath caught in his chest when Elizabeth slid her hand through the crook of his elbow and they walked the last few steps along the Longbourn drive not as strangers or enemies, but as friends.

"Lizzy, is that you?" Mr Bennet called from his study.

"It is, Papa, and I have brought a guest!"

"Oh?" There was the sound of a chair scraping across floorboards, much shuffling of piled books and detritus and a few swallowed curses before Mr Bennet's head appeared in the doorway, blinking in confusion as he fixed his gaze on Mr Darcy. "Aha. Mr Darcy. What brings you here?"

The greeting was not cool, exactly, but it certainly lacked the warmth the Bennet patriarch might have offered towards certain other guests. *Like my cousin.* Darcy swallowed. He had managed to put all thoughts of Richard - both good and bad - aside, allowing himself to enjoy a stolen half-hour with Elizabeth Bennet. The break had done him good, and for the first time since his return to Hertfordshire, he had felt the clouds that hung over him lift. They returned, full-force, with the reminder that of the two cousins, he was not the one most readily welcomed under this roof.

*Well, you have not lost the opportunity to change that*, he thought, forcing his uncooperative lips to curve upwards in a smile.

"It has been suggested to me that I might like to stay for a spot of tea. Will you join us, Mr Bennet?"

Mr Bennet's eyes narrowed and he opened his mouth as if to say something about the incredulity of being invited to take tea in his own house by a man who did not live here, but his gaze travelled to Lizzy and something he saw there prompted him to swallow his comment.

"Indeed. Go on into the parlour. I shall join you."

He waited until they had progressed past his door - past any hope of safety or escape, Darcy thought - before calling after them.

"You shall be a welcome addition, I am sure, Mr Darcy, for Lydia, Kitty and Mary have all been hovering around Jane and my wife all morning. They are surely eager for a fresh victim."

Darcy could hear laughter in the older man's voice but had no time to do anything but press a vague smile onto his features as Elizabeth opened the door to the parlour and ushered him inside.

"Lizzy!" Jane exclaimed, looking up from her embroidery. Her eyes widened slightly as she realised her sister was not alone. "And...Mr Darcy!"

Four other feminine heads swivelled towards him, eyes opening in mirrored surprise, and he struggled to keep his smile in place.

"Good morning, ladies." He snatched his hat off his head and bowed, feeling Lizzy slip free of him and saunter over to peer at her sister's embroidery, leaving him to face the rest of her family alone. They all blinked up at him, expectantly and he hurried out an explanation that sounded as unbelievable as it was true.

"I happened to be walking not too far from here and crossed paths with Miss Elizabeth. It seemed only right to ensure that she reached home safely."

"Of course," Lydia exclaimed, her eyes bright with amusement. "Very chivalrous."

"Noble, I should say." Kitty swallowed a giggle.

Darcy could feel his cheeks reddening and turned back towards the open door just in time to see the hallway blocked by Mr Bennet's bulk.

"Well, I think it a kindness. You often bestowed the same on me in London and I shall never forget it," Mary said, loyally. She shot her younger sisters a quelling look before turning back to Mr Darcy with a bright smile. "Won't you sit down?"

"Yes, do sit down, Mr Darcy," Mrs Bennet gushed, pushing her daughters aside in her eagerness to welcome their handsome, newly-returned neighbour. "I hope Lizzy did not drag you on a route march on your way here." She glared at her. "You must be quite worn out."

"Mama!" Lizzy laughed. "You make me sound like some kind of drill-sergeant. Might I remind you that Mr Darcy was already out walking when our paths crossed? And that he offered to walk the rest of the way here entirely off his own back."

Lydia and Kitty dissolved into whispers and giggles that made Darcy sink, as unobtrusively as possible, into a chair. He might be growing slowly acclimatised to his interest in Elizabeth Bennet, but that did not mean he wished it - or himself - to become an object of ridicule.

"What are you two giggling about?" Mr Bennet complained, coming in at last to join them. "If there's one thing I cannot abide it is giggling. Cease and desist!" He spoke gruffly but his eyes sparkled with humour and affection, and he took deliberate consideration of where to sit, at last deciding upon a chair near to Darcy, offering him a silent show of support that was only too necessary.

"You must not mind my daughters, Mr Darcy. Far too silly for their own good, every one." He swept an arm in a wide arc, encompassing the whole room until it came to rest on Lizzy's shoulder, which he patted warmly. "Except for Lizzy, of course. She is by far the most sensible..."

"The cleverest!" Lydia put in, sourly.

"The most charming!" Kitty mimicked.

"The one who certainly does not deserve to be singled out, when Jane is sitting next to her!" Elizbeth declared, tweaking a lock of Jane's blonde hair, and turning their conversation in a new direction.

Darcy watched her, pleased to be afforded a moment of quiet where he need not be the centre of attention. How could he ever have nursed anything but affection for Elizabeth? He marvelled at the way he had dismissed her, upon their first meeting, and dared to think that by leaving Hertfordshire for London he would be leaving her behind. *Why did I ever wish to?* he asked himself, his heart sinking uncomfortably in his chest. *I know I shall never be able to be without her, if only I had the slightest hope she might feel the same...*

# Chapter Ten

A good part of the day had passed by the time Darcy made his way back to Netherfield, but he did not regret it. He had enjoyed his walk with Elizabeth far more than he had a right to, with things still so at odds between him and his cousin. What was more, Elizabeth had seemed to enjoy walking with him. That thought lifted his spirits, buoying him along the last few yards towards home. He would mend things with Richard today, he thought, and not allow matters to fester any longer. There would be some explanation, surely, some reason for Richard's apparent friendliness with George Wickham. Darcy's smile faded. Again, Wickham was causing him strife merely by existing on the periphery of his life, and again, Darcy had allowed the man free rein over his thoughts. He shook his head. *No more.*

Forcibly returning his mind to thoughts of Elizabeth, he was still smiling as he crossed the threshold of Netherfield Park, but he came to a sudden stop with the realisation that the house was not deserted, as it had been when he had left it. He could hear voices. Not the hushed, whispered conversations that took place between servants as they worked, but the raised, comfortable voices of people who felt entirely at home.

*Did someone call?* Darcy could count on one hand the people he knew well enough in Meryton to imagine them calling on him at home and the majority of those people he had left behind him at Longbourn. He was sure of it. Then who...?

"Mr Darcy!"

Caroline Bingley had spotted him first, leaping to her feet and scurrying across the Netherfield parlour to greet him.

"Thank goodness you are here! You can talk some sense into my brother!" Her eyebrows drew together in a frown but she was visibly concerned about Charles who, Darcy could see now, was pale and agitated, stalking back and forwards before the fire like a caged animal.

"What are you -"

Darcy did not complete his question before he acknowledged a third figure in the large, airy parlour. His heart sank into his boots and he prayed his disappointment was not evident in his voice.

"Georgiana."

"You mustn't mind me coming, William," she said, evidently anticipating his protests and heading them off at the pass. "I could hardly let Caroline come without support. Not when her brother is -"

"Is what?" Charles asked, turning wildly towards Georgiana, his eyes flashing with more emotion than Darcy had ever seen there before. "I know you have been discussing me, you and Caroline. Well, do not keep your opinions to yourself." He spun around to face Caroline and Darcy, his eyes blazing with emotion. "I am irrational, I suppose? I am acting too hastily." He shook his head. "There is no degree of haste *too much*. And I certainly mean to avoid listening to your advice in future, Caroline. It is your fault I left Hertfordshire, to begin with. If I had not..."

He sagged, then, all the fight flowing out of him, and gripped hold of the mantelpiece to steady himself.

Darcy went straight to his side, guiding him into a chair.

"You look exhausted," he remarked, to nobody in particular. "When did you arrive? Have you eaten?"

He could not bring himself to look at Georgiana but addressed his comments to the entire room.

"Yes, we must eat something." Caroline was eager to have some occupation and busied herself in requesting some refreshments be brought to the parlour, slipping out of the room long enough for Georgiana to slip silently to Darcy's side.

"I meant to help -" she began.

"I told you to remain in London." Darcy's voice was cold and he knew Georgiana was hurt by it. She recoiled, the light in her eyes dimming, and he instantly regretted not keeping himself in better check. He drew in a breath and tried again. "This is a mess, Georgie. I do not know -"

"Damned right it is a mess!" Charles grumbled from his chair. "You ought to have written to me sooner, Darcy. I have been going half-mad waiting to hear from you. Is it any wonder I came as soon as I received word that it is true? That my Jane is - is betrothed." He spat out the word as if he could not bear the taste of it and Georgiana and Darcy exchanged a look.

"How is Jane?" Georgiana asked, addressing her words in a whisper she hoped would not carry to Bingley's ears. "And how is Richard?"

"They are both well," Darcy said, shortly. "By all accounts well and happy."

"Accounts?" Georgiana frowned. "Then you have not seen them?"

"Here we are!" Caroline cooed, throwing open the door to a procession of servants who brought what seemed like half of the Netherfield pantry up to offer to their newly-arrived guests. "I think it best we follow your wise advice, Mr Darcy, and take some refreshments before we go any further with anything." Her eyes flitted to her brother, concern etched into her face. "Charles, you will feel much better once you have eaten."

"I am not hungry." Charles scowled, but obediently accepted the tea Caroline poured for him and drank half a cup down without protest. He soon moved onto a small slice of fruit cake and then began heaping his plate with food, eating as if he had not done for days.

"Will you take a cup of tea, Mr Darcy?" Caroline asked, pouring him one anyway and striding over to where he stood, observing his friend from a distance. She thrust the cup into his hand but did not immediately let go, forcing him to meet her gaze.

"My brother is distraught," she whispered, her back to Charles and her words designed to be heard by only Darcy. "He has come to challenge Colonel Fitzwilliam." Her voice dropped still lower so that she ended up merely mouthing the words. "To a duel."

"A duel?" Darcy flinched, spilling tea over the side of his cup and scalding his thumb. He swallowed a curse, and let go of his hold on the cup, turning to Charles. "You can't be serious."

"I can and I am," Charles said, with a business-like nod. He continued to eat with vigour, his words muffled with chewing.

"Fitzwilliam has acted abominably and needs to be brought to task. I know he is your cousin, but -"

"He is also far better at pistols than you," Georgiana ventured, dropping to her knees beside Charles's chair and clinging pleadingly to his arm. "Be sensible, Charles. It is not worth an injury -"

"I am tired of being told what I must do by ladies who think they know better," Charles retorted, shaking off Georgiana's grip and ignoring her pleas. He turned to Darcy, fixing his eyes on his friend with surprising calm. "I only come to you first, Darcy, to see if you will be my second. There's nobody I trust more with my life."

Darcy swallowed, considering the gravity of his friend's question. To second anybody in a duel was a large ask, but to be pitted against his own cousin?

"Please, Mr Darcy," Caroline asked, her voice tremulous with tears. "If there is anybody who can help us, it is you. Please do not refuse us now."

"YOU HAVE LEFT YOUR queen open," Mr Bennet remarked, as he surveyed the chess board that sat between him and Colonel Fitzwilliam. When he received no reply he continued, stroking his chin as he surveyed the game. "I only mention it because it is a simple error and surely a deliberate choice. A tactician such as yourself would never leave such a space unless he planned to. You intend to trap me, no doubt." His fingertips hovered over his pieces and at last, he made a trifling move that gained him little but cost nothing.

Richard nodded, moving another piece of his own into direct danger, whereupon Mr Bennet easily subsumed it, and checkmated Richard in one move, ending their game.

"Very good," Richard muttered, arranging the pieces back on their starting squares. "Another?"

Mr Bennet paused, looking with concern at his younger friend.

"Your heart is not in it, I wager."

Richard's head darted up.

"Mine?" He smiled, broadly and easily. "I suppose I was not fully engaged, but that does not mean I shall remain so." He cracked his knuckles. "Let us try again, Mr Bennet, and see how my heart fares."

He could hear the hollowness in his voice but hoped his companion did not. He wagered wrongly, though, for Mr Bennet was a good deal more insightful than Richard ever gave him credit for.

Mr Bennet did not move, merely folded his hands and waited patiently for Richard to share a little more. And at length, he did, leaning back in his chair and lifting one of his knights to admire its carving.

"I suppose I am a little distracted," he conceded. "I exchanged words with someone last evening and the matter is not resolved." He placed the chess piece back down carefully and shrugged one shoulder. "I miss the ease of life at the front. Disagreements are resolved in a swift exchange of blows and by the end of the evening one can be drinking again as old friends."

"Not a course of action I would advise here," Mr Bennet remarked, raising his brows.

"No." Richard laughed. "Certainly not."

"However much one might wish to..." Mr Bennet pursed his lips. "Exchange blows. After all, the other fellow might do a better job at it than you, and you do not wish to wear a black eye in the run-up to your wedding."

"Doubtful on both counts!" Richard replied, his spirits lifting at the thought of Darcy besting him by any degree in an altercation. His smile dropped when he recalled how dismissive his cousin had been last evening. He had trusted Darcy, valued him as a friend, almost as a brother. *Closer than my brother*, he thought, bitterly. *And how easily he turned on me at the very thought that I was showing Wickham anything like friendship.* His blood ran cold in his veins. How much worse would matters turn if Darcy ever discovered the truth, that he, Richard, had been the one to first introduce Wickham to Georgiana?

"Conversation often produces similar results," Mr Bennet continued, with a twinkle in his eye. "Without half so many bruises."

Richard harrumphed. He would not go cap in hand seeking his cousin out. He wished to make things right, but he certainly was not about to trample his pride into the ground to do so. He could be just as aloof as his cousin when he chose to be.

"Mr Darcy called here this morning," Mr Bennet remarked, after a long moment of silence. Richard's scowl darkened, all the answer his friend needed that the rift to which Richard referred was between the two cousins.

"He seemed quite unlike himself."

"That is not my fault. If he chooses -"

"He was smiling." Mr Bennet raised his eyebrows. "Quite cheerful. Although I dare say, were the conversation to turn to you, that would have changed. Why not mend fences with him now, before things become even more strained between the two of you?"

"If he is unfazed by our disagreement I do not see why I must mend anything," Richard grumbled, hearing his voice and cringing at how childish he sounded. Mr Bennet was to one day become his father-in-law, after all. He wished to impress him, not to display his intransigence. He straightened, taking a deep breath. "But I dare say you are right and I must make my peace." He surveyed the chess set. "And I shall do, but not before you've given me a chance to win back a little of my reputation. Come, let's have another game and I shall deploy every one of my wits this time."

"You needn't," Mr Bennet countered, making the first move and awaiting Richard's. "I stand half a chance of winning when you are distracted."

The game was an enjoyable one and ended in a stalemate, so for once both players were satisfied. Snatching up his hat, Richard bade his friend farewell and made his way out of Longbourn, stopping at the parlour to pass a short greeting with Mrs Bennet and Mary, who were sitting together in peaceable quiet.

"Jane is not here," Mary offered, looking up from her book with a disappointed smile. "She will be sorry to have missed you!"

"I'm sure." Richard grinned. "Well, I shall leave it to you to pass on my greetings, then, Miss Mary. To each of your sisters." He winked. "Tell them I said something devilishly entertaining and they ought to repent of not being here to hear it." He bowed. "Good afternoon, Mrs Bennet."

"Oh, good day, Colonel Fitzwilliam. Are we to expect you at dinner?"

"Not this evening," Richard said, with an apologetic smile. "I am on duty."

"Again?" She pouted. "We hardly see you!"

"You see a good deal too much of me, I am sure." Richard chuckled "I do not wish you all to be sick of me before the wedding even arrives!" He bade both ladies adieu and made his way out of the house, chuckling as Mrs Bennet called after him.

"We could never tire of you! We shall tell poor Jane that she missed you! Come again soon, won't you?"

His mood was a good deal improved by his short visit to Longbourn, and he thanked heaven for providing a firm friend in Mr Bennet as well as a soon-to-be wife in Jane. He marvelled to think how vastly different his life was from what it had been but a few short weeks ago.

*And it will be different again a few short weeks from now*, he reminded himself. *Once Jane and I are married.*

His smile faltered. He could not quite embrace the future ahead of him with the knowledge that he and Darcy were at odds. Despite his bravado with Mr Bennet, he knew how unlikely it was that Darcy would ever seek him out for an apology.

*Better I make the first move*, he thought, ramming his hat onto his head and altering his course directly across the fields towards Netherfield. He had time to spare, now, to make the call, and the three-mile walk would be quite sufficient for him to order his thoughts. *I shall be honest*, he told himself. *I shall tell Darcy all - everything that has occurred between Wickham and I. He might not forgive me, but at least then he will know.* His blood ran cold at the thought that Darcy - his friend as well as his cousin - might be irretrievably removed from him, but he could not linger in indecision. Better the truth be laid out there, and then they could move on, friends or not. *It is not as if I am ill-practised at being estranged from my family,* he thought, with a grim recollection of his last visit to his brother. *I have survived thus far: I will survive this.*

But the thought was not a happy one, and his spirits sank with every stride he took towards Netherfield.

# Chapter Eleven

"This is my favourite place in all of Hertfordshire!" Lizzy exclaimed, tilting her face up towards the spring sunshine and smiling, happily.

"You said that about the brook, the way it weaves through the trees in the Appledown clearing," Jane pointed out. "And the tumble-down bridge we pass on the way to Meryton. And our very own library..."

"Very well, this is my favourite place *today*," Lizzy conceded with a laugh. She opened her eyes, drinking in the sight of the tree blossoms dancing in the sunlight. "Isn't it beautiful? Aren't we lucky to have such a place as this?"

"Yes." Jane's answer was genuine, but her smile did not quite reach her eyes. Lizzy stooped to pick a daisy that was growing near her feet and absently plucked its petals one at a time, girding her courage to being the conversation she wished to have with her sister. It was not about blossom that she wished to talk, or sunshine, but Mr Darcy. Heat flooded her cheeks and she turned away, grateful that Jane chanced not to be looking at her at that moment.

"I am surprised you wished to come here with me," Lizzy remarked, after a long moment of silence between the two sisters. "Lately it is impossible to persuade you to come on even the shortest of walks."

"What is a *short walk* to you is a test of endurance to the rest of us." Jane raised her eyebrows. "I have confirmed as much with Richard. Even he agrees it is asking a lot to expect company when you decide to roam half of Hertfordshire and call it fun."

Elizabeth laughed, picturing the wry smile Colone Fitzwilliam would wear when he made such a statement. She conceded the point with a dainty curtsey.

"In any case, if one of us had been with you walking this morning you would never have had Mr Darcy for company." Jane's gaze met Elizabeth's, brimming with curiosity and concern.

Lizzy's heart began to beat quickly in her chest. This, then, was the very opportunity she had longed for. She could speak quite openly of Mr Darcy now, and it had not been down to her to be the first to mention him.

"It was kind of him to escort me all the way home, do not you think?" Elizabeth strove for nonchalance but even she could hear a peculiar note of anxiety in her voice. She swallowed and tried again, praying that she would sound normal to her sister's ears, if not her own. "And I have never known him to smile or laugh as much as he did this morning. Do you know, Jane, I think him quite altered by his time in London."

"You certainly seem altered in your opinions of him." Jane's response was sage, the very kind of detached observation Lizzy herself might have made, and for a moment it felt as if the sisters' role had been reversed. Lizzy was the flighty romantic and Jane the rational one of the two.

"Am I wrong to change my mind?" Lizzy plucked the last petals from her daisy and discarded it, dropping her arms to her sides. "Very well, let me be wrong." She bit her lip, strangely nervous to confide this truth in the sister she loved and trusted above all others. "I think - I think him very amiable, very clever and -" She swallowed. "Well, I have never claimed I did not think him handsome." With a yelp, she buried her head in her hands, muffling the last of her confession. "There is no hope for me, Jane. I think I love him!"

To her surprise, Jane did not leap back in shock at this surprising admission. She made no response at all, and Lizzy peeked at her from between two fingers. Jane was not looking at her, but her brow was furrowed as if in thought and at first Lizzy wondered if she had heard her at all.

"Jane?" she ventured, lifting her head just enough to see without squinting. "Well, Jane? Tease me if you must. I dare say I deserve it!"

"You care for Mr Darcy?" Jane shrugged her thin shoulders. "I do not see why your acknowledgement of that should lead to teasing."

Lizzy's mouth fell open in shock.

"It does not seem to lead to surprise, either." She frowned. "Jane, you act as if you knew all along that I cared for Mr Darcy. How can you when I have only just realised the truth myself!"

Jane smiled, then, her old, knowing smile. She slipped an arm around her sister and together they continued their amble through the orchard.

"You act surprised that anyone should know a thing about you before you do. Has it never occurred to you that you are not the most aware of your own feelings? The grudge you bore against Mr Darcy's first slight against you was an indication to us all that you cared more for him than you claimed. If you did not like him why should it matter what he said or thought of you?"

Lizzy groaned, burying her head in her sister's shoulder.

"Then you have all been laughing at me, all this time?"

"Hardly." Jane shook her head. "I do not suppose the others noticed. Mary, maybe. But Lydia and Kitty are too preoccupied with their own interests to care for anyone else's."

"I did not like him at first," Lizzy said, straightening and slipping free of her sister's arm to stoop and pluck another daisy. Her hands needed some occupation and destruction offered her the perfect distraction from sharing what was on her heart and had been until now - at least as far as she was aware - private. "He was so proud! And the way he parted you and Mr Bingley!"

Jane stiffened.

"I'm sorry!" Lizzy said at once. "I did not mean to mention his name." She paused. "Perhaps it was for the best! After all, without Mr Bingley going away you would never have met Colonel Fitzwilliam and now look how happy you are!"

"Yes, I am happy."

Jane looked into the middle distance, her smile strangely sad, but before Lizzy could query it, she brightened, turning to her sister with a merry smile.

"Now you must tell me every detail of your conversation with Mr Darcy this morning! For I dare say it was this that has gone a long way in changing your mind about him. Was he *so* charming and *so* chivalrous - ouch!"

Jane yelped as Lizzy jabbed her in the side, and laughing, they continued to walk and talk and share secrets, happy in the revival of their sisterly closeness, in the sunshine and surrounded by the fragrant beauty of the cherry blossom.

THE NETHERFIELD PARLOUR was silent but for the ticking of the clock on the mantel. Ordinarily, Darcy found the quiet comforting but that afternoon the tension was so thick that silence merely kept his already frayed nerves perpetually on edge.

"Perhaps -" Caroline began to speak, but hurriedly swallowed the rest of her sentence at the glare her brother shot her.

Darcy drew a breath, wondering who, if any of them, might be able to break the silent stalemate that had fallen over the room. He was spared the challenge of trying, however, because there was a knock at the parlour door, which opened immediately to admit a servant who skirted Bingley altogether, going straight to Darcy's right-hand side. If Bingley took a slight from being thus ignored in the house that was technically his, he did not show it, and whilst Caroline might ordinarily have reacted angrily, she was too concerned with her brother to notice.

"Sir, you have a caller..." The servant kept his voice quiet, shooting a glance over his shoulder that betrayed he was particularly careful of not being overheard by the newest arrivals. "It is Colonel Fitzwilliam."

Darcy straightened, casting a concerned glance at his friend, but the servant did his job well, keeping his voice a low whisper that did not carry.

"I have shown him into the study, sir, thinking it best you meet him there."

"Indeed!" Darcy stood, pacing a quick retreat towards the door with the servant in tow. "Quite right." He paused at the threshold, glancing back towards his friends, who scarcely seemed to notice he had moved. Charles continued to glare fiercely towards the fireplace, stewing over the wrongs that had been done to him, and Caroline and Georgiana both watched him helplessly.

With reluctance, and a pressing wish to meet and dismiss his cousin as soon as possible, Darcy hurried along the corridor to the study and pushed the door open, finding Richard standing to attention before the fire.

"Darcy."

He did not smile, and Darcy felt again the chill of estrangement that had crept up between them. *I am not to blame for that!* he recalled, taking a seat and wordlessly gesturing his cousin to another.

"Am I not welcome in the parlour now?" Richard's voice was cool, but Darcy thought he could sense genuine hurt in his cousin's eyes.

"I much prefer to meet you here," Darcy said, taking care to push the door closed. "Where we might have privacy."

"Privacy?" Richard smirked, taking the chair Darcy had pointed to. "From whom? Ah, but I shall not question Fitzwilliam Darcy on modes of etiquette. There is sure to be some fine reason behind your actions that a rough colonel cannot begin to grasp."

Darcy said nothing, but steepled his hands and stared past them at his cousin in silence. For a long moment, neither gentleman said a word.

"What do you want, Richard?"

It was Darcy who spoke, at last, rueing the sharpness of his voice in the otherwise quiet room. It made the request sound more like censure than he meant it to, and Richard stiffened, any ounce of amiability in his manner dropping completely.

"I came to call on my cousin at home. And to mend fences after our disagreement last evening." He muttered something else under his breath, casting a dismal look at the fire, and in the end seemed to come to some unspoken agreement within himself. He stood, striding towards the door. "I see now I have made a mistake in doing so. Fear not, Darcy, I know when I am not wanted."

He strode out into the hallway, leaving the door to the small study wide open behind him, and Darcy did not let go of the breath he held until Richard's sharp footsteps retreated into silence.

*That solved nothing.* He rubbed his forehead, the scowl sliding back into place and hiding a headache he could already feel forming. Richard had tried to make amends, perhaps even to explain himself, and Darcy had denied him even the chance of reconciliation.

*I did not prevent it altogether*, he reasoned. *Richard might have said anything in his defence and I would have listened.* All told, though, he could not mourn the fact that his cousin was safely gone from Netherfield and safe from Charles Bingley, at least for a little while longer. He did not yet know how he was going to dissuade his friend from pursuing his claim against Richard. A duel would spell disaster, for Darcy did not doubt Richard's prowess with a rifle, but he certainly did not wish to be caught between the two duellers. If only he had not written to Charles! But this, too, was a vain hope. His friend would have come having heard nothing, just as eagerly as he had come after receiving Darcy's letter, he knew that. But had his deliberate mention of Richard been the fuse to Bingley's rarely seen anger?

"Darcy?"

It was Georgiana's voice that called to him and Darcy stood, rearranging his features into a smile just in time for her to knock lightly at the open study door, stepping inside cautiously.

"Oh, you are alone! Good." She smiled with relief.

Darcy nodded, saying nothing. He had not managed to make sense of the conflict between Bingley and Colonel Fitzwilliam, nor think how to resolve it. He had not imagination spare to consider how best to handle Georgiana's presence in Meryton, and Wickham still so close by.

"Do not look so seriously at me," Georgiana warned. "I know you are poised to tell me I ought to have remained in London and I shall simply demand to know what good I could have done there, with all this chaos going on here?"

"Chaos?" Darcy asked, wryly. "Is that what this is?"

"You have a better word?" Georgiana smiled, tightly. "But together I am sure we can puzzle out a solution." Her breath caught and she glanced over her shoulder. "And it is for that reason I came to find you. Charles - that is, Mr Bingley - is eager to ride over to Netherfield and see Miss Bennet. I offered to go with him. I don't think it wise he go alone, not when he is so out of temper, and Miss Bingley is too tired to make the journey, she says. I wondered..." She looked at him with eyes bigger than usual. "Might you be persuaded to come with us?"

Darcy's heart sank. What he wouldn't give to acquiesce to Georgiana's request! He could see Elizabeth again, who, despite all that surrounded him, was never far from his thoughts. He could ensure Bingley not say or do a thing he regretted. He could have the joy of seeing his sister welcomed and well-liked - for how could she not be - by a whole family of friends.

"Very well," he said, at last, his voice little more than a sigh. "Let us go now, and perhaps between us we can keep Charles from making an even greater fool of himself than he has already."

# Chapter Twelve

"This is not the way to Longbourn," Charles grumbled, when the Netherfield carriage turned yet another corner and succeeded in taking them the long, diverted circuit Darcy had outlined to their driver.

"We shall arrive presently," Darcy reassured him, exchanging a look with his sister. The scheme had been devised between them, to get Charles out into the world again but not take him immediately to Longbourn, where he was certain to cause upset to himself and Jane Bennet's whole family.

"How pleasant this countryside is!" Georgiana remarked, her voice and smile doing the hard work of elevating the stormy mood inside the carriage. "I see now why you were eager to return."

Darcy was not sure if this was directed towards him or Bingley, but as the latter's scowl merely deepened, he threw himself into the breach with an answer.

"It is not Derbyshire, but certainly far prettier than London."

"And you must tell me about Meryton," Georgiana continued, with a desperate look at Bingley. She hoped that the longer they travelled and the louder they talked they might somehow exhaust Charles Bingley completely and persuade him out of his foolhardy errand. "Is it quite large?"

"Compared to London?" Darcy opened his mouth to respond further but before he could, Charles had commented, his voice lacking its usual brightness but with at least a spark of interest.

"We might go there first, I suppose." He wrenched his gaze away from the window to look at each of his friends in turn. "I know you are trying to distract me from calling on Jane in hopes I will forget. I shan't, but perhaps you are right in that I needn't go there right away. If Georgiana wishes to see Meryton, let us go to Meryton."

Darcy opened his mouth to protest. The very last place he wished to take Georgiana was to Meryton, where she would be within walking distance, perhaps even within sight, of the barracks. How could he possibly keep her from being reunited with George Wickham?

*He will be working*, he reassured himself. *And we need not stay long.*

He hesitated too long in offering a counter-argument, even if he could have thought one up, for Georgiana's face lit up at the suggestion of Meryton, and before Darcy could say another word their instructions were relayed to the driver and the carriage changed course, lurching along the road that would lead them to town.

"We shall just take a short tour," Bingley said, growing more like himself with every turn of the carriage wheel. "Perhaps I shall purchase some flowers. I suppose it will be better to arrive with a gift than to turn up empty-handed, eh, Darcy?"

He smiled - the first genuine smile Darcy had seen on his friend's face since the party's arrival from London and quite some time before. Darcy managed only a grimace in return.

"I should like to see all the places I heard Mary talk about," Georgiana exclaimed, turning a rapt expression towards the window so that she might be first to glimpse Meryton's main street of shops and see if the reality matched the picture she had conjured in her imagination.

"I do not imagine she had so very much to say about the place," Darcy replied, tight-lipped. "As far as I recall, you spent most of your time talking about music."

"That shows what you know!" Georgiana teased, her eyes rolling. "As if two young ladies could have nothing of interest to discuss except music. We talked about her family, for you know I am always eager to know people, and about her home." She smiled. "I told her about Pemberley, too, of course."

"Of course." Darcy shifted uncomfortably in his seat, not entirely pleased with this intelligence. How often had he been a feature of his sister's conversation? How often had Elizabeth been a topic of Mary's? He frowned, considering the matter, and was distracted enough from his sister's eager chatter that he almost did not hear her trilling observation.

"Oh, is that the barracks?"

Silence swept through the carriage interior, and Georgiana realised too late her mistake.

"No, I am mistaken. It is surely just a building. Oh, look! A book-binders. We must stop there, William."

Bingley's features, which had almost been lightened to a smile, folded once more into a scowl that looked quite unnatural on his fair and amiable face.

"I suppose I might call at the barracks just as easily as Longbourn, and have a resolution to this mess," he growled, stopping only when Georgiana turned and laid a pleading hand on his arm.

"Don't!" Her voice trembled with anxiety. "Please don't! Richard is my cousin, and you are my friend, and I do not -"

"You can hardly do anything until you have spoken to Miss Bennet," Darcy said, cagily. "What good will it serve you to call out her fiancé if she truly spares no more affection for you? You will make enemies on all sides."

It was a bargain Darcy was making. He knew there would be a confrontation before long, one way or another, however much he wished to avoid it. If only he could keep it from taking place today, and keep it from happening at a barracks where more problems than those between Charles Bingley and Richard Fitzwilliam might erupt.

"You wished to buy flowers," he reminded his friend. "Let's make that our aim. I am sure you, like I, could stand to walk a few steps and as Georgiana is fond of reminding me, one can never truly appreciate a place from inside a carriage."

His voice was pleading in a way it did not often need to be with Charles Bingley, and it seemed to work, for his friend's scowl held out only a moment longer.

"Very well," he whispered, unclenching his jaw and attempting to smile. He patted Georgiana's hand warmly with his own. "Don't fret, Georgie. I shall not act rashly any more today."

Georgiana let out a relieved sigh, her gaze meeting Darcy's and mirroring his disbelief. They had avoided two *rash acts* already and Bingley had been back in Hertfordshire only a couple of hours.

*And I fear we have merely delayed, not averted, future disaster*, Darcy reflected, feeling his heart-rate slow to something approaching normal as the carriage put the barracks behind them and continued to their destination.

RICHARD'S STUDY AT the Meryton barracks was small. That fact had never bothered him before. He was stoical and self-contained and saw no need for acres of space. Besides which, to have a room at all was a step-up from sleeping under canvas, and he had rather valued having a small, quiet space with which to withdraw, attend to his responsibilities and be alone.

That afternoon, however, he was certain the very walls were closing in on him.

A knock at the door made him look up from the letter he was writing so suddenly he spilt a drop of ink on the page. Cursing, he tried to blot away the worst of it and barked a terse response.

"Yes?"

The door swung open and George Wickham strolled in, beaming and oblivious to Richard's annoyance.

"What do you want?" Richard asked, wearily. He looked down at his letter, preferring to focus on that than Wickham's smug grin, and relishing the fact that it proved he was, in fact, busy and had no time to devote to whatever nonsense was top of Wickham's mind.

"I came to see how you are faring."

Wickham slid into the chair Richard did not offer him and leaned forward, peering at the ink-stained correspondence and noticing the agitation in his friend's movements.

"Not well, it seems."

"As ever you are adept in observing that which you have no business observing." Richard finished his letter quickly, signing it with a flourish and setting it aside. "And I know for a fact you have no human concern for any but yourself, so you need not act as if you are here only to enquire after my wellbeing." Richard winced at the word. He had been beyond *well* only a day previously. He had been happy. Thrilled at the thought of the future which awaited him and on good terms with everyone he met. *Until Darcy came back*. With him, his cousin had brought the striking reminder that Richard's *wellbeing with the world* would only last as long as his association with George Wickham remained concealed, and there had been an abject failure on his part to do just that.

"Very well," Wickham said, business-like at once. "I came to find out whether you have heard the same rumour I have heard." He drew a breath. "If you might be able to confirm whether it is fact or fiction." He leaned back in his chair, folding his hands together and fixing his gaze expectantly on Richard.

"What?" Richard groaned at last, knowing he could not help asking but furious with himself all the same. He had fallen right into Wickham's trap. *Again*.

"News abroad is that Charles Bingley is back at Netherfield Park."

"Well, that is a lie." Richard shrugged his broad shoulders. "I was there just today and saw nobody but my cousin..." He trailed off, as a second and then a third thought occurred to him. He had seen nobody but Darcy, that was true, but he had not exactly been welcomed there. His access to the property had been limited to the study, and Darcy had come to him, never once suggesting they move to another room. Who was to say Charles Bingley had not been there, enjoying the comforts of the parlour while Richard was relegated to the study and hurried away again like a shameful intruder.

Wickham was watching him carefully and could not fail to have noticed the shadows that flickered across Richard's face as he considered all this. His lips quirked into a smile.

"According to my source, a carriage came hurrying back from London carrying Mr Bingley and his sister. Now, what do you suppose could be the reason for his sudden return?"

"I dare say he grew tired of London and missed Netherfield," Richard said, wearily.

"I say rather he had cause to hurry back when he heard of a certain engagement."

Richard frowned, looking up at him in disbelief.

"What should it matter to Charles Bingley to hear I am engaged? We are not close friends. I barely know the man."

"I concede it is likely he cares little to hear of your engagement in the abstract." Wickham's smile grew cruel. "But there is the small matter of who you have become engaged *to.*"

Richard was still gripping tight hold of his quill-pen and forced himself to let go, lest he snap the thing in two. It dropped with a clatter onto the desk.

"He is acquainted with Jane? Well, why would he not be? They are neighbours."

"Rumour has it the two were more than a little acquainted." Wickham took great care in examining his nails, only too aware of the torture he was inflicting upon Richard by dropping tiny snatches of information like breadcrumbs. "People say there was an expectation that they would marry before he disappeared off to London at Christmas."

A muscle twitched in Richard's jaw. He could not be surprised by this news, surely? He certainly was not about to admit as much before George Wickham, in any case. Of course Jane had known people before him. And she was so beautiful, so elegant, so charming that it was unfathomable to think there had not been beaux in her past.

"Clearly, they reached no agreement," he ground out, praying Wickham would not sense how much of an effort it took for him to speak quietly, calmly, with a measure of peace he did not feel. "Jane was free to accept me, or not."

"Aye." Wickham nodded, sagely. "But I dare say she did not ever expect to see Charles Bingley again."

Richard's eyes narrowed, dangerously.

"You mean to suggest that she will break our engagement simply because he has come back to Netherfield? Take care, Wickham. You speak with complete disregard to a lady's character, and that will not be without consequence."

"Be calm, Richard!" Wickham chuckled. "I am not so impertinent as all that. I merely came to pose a question to you, if it is indeed true that Charles Bingley has hastened himself back here on account of things between you and Miss Bennet..." He paused. "Where do you suppose he might have learned of your engagement? Who do you think has summoned him back here? Spite, I call it..."

Richard's blood flashed hot in his veins. *Darcy*. No wonder his cousin had been avoiding him, reluctant to make up their argument of the other day. He bore a grudge over Wickham, but to seek to destroy the only happiness Richard had ever known...

Wickham spoke again, his voice smooth and tempting.

"You know I have your back no matter what. We have been through enough together, you and I..."

"You speak as if we are friends, Wickham. We are not friends. We work together now only because we must and be assured if I had the power to dismiss you, I would. Do not presume to know me, or to know what assistance I require -"

"Do you have friends enough that you can afford to discard me?" Wickham was serious now and drove his point home with bitter accuracy. "Your own cousin's loyalty seems questionable at best." He smiled, grimly. "But fear not. I will support you, whatever should happen next. You can trust me."

# Chapter Thirteen

Darcy did not fully begin to breathe easily until he, Georgiana and Charles were once again inside their carriage and heading towards home. Thus far, he had avoided disaster on two fronts: Georgiana had been kept safe from seeing George Wickham, and Charles had been distracted from calling immediately on Jane Bennet. He drew in a breath. *Three fronts.* Charles had also been prevented from demanding an interview with Colonel Fitzwilliam, which would have undoubtedly escalated matters not only between them but between Darcy and his cousin. A sharp pain started to make its presence felt in his head and he massaged at a spot on his forehead as if that might ease the tension. It did little but call attention to it.

"Are you unwell, William?" Georgiana's voice was all concern and Darcy immediately straightened, plastering a smile on his face that he doubted was at all convincing.

"Quite well." He swallowed, glancing at Bingley, whose own gaze remained fixed, unseeing, on the scenery they passed, his features unreadable. "A little tired."

"Better we go straight home, then," Georgiana ventured, her voice loud enough that it must have carried to Bingley's ears, although he made no sign that he had heard her.

Nobody said anything for a moment, until Georgiana kicked Darcy unceremoniously, across the expansive interior of the carriage. He winced and she glared at him, accompanying the kick with a silent instruction that he say something.

*What?* he thought, desperately. *When have my words ever succeeded in improving things where matters of the heart are concerned?* Georgiana did not know, of course. She could not know that during his short tenure in Hertfordshire, Darcy had caused more problems by speaking than by staying silent, and he had learnt to favour the latter, especially where his friend Charles was concerned.

Still, saying nothing would be tantamount to encouragement, in this case. He would do anything, now, to keep from calling at Longbourn that afternoon. With an evening of reflection, Charles might be persuaded to think otherwise, or at least to act otherwise. Confrontation might be avoided for another day.

*And what of Richard?* Darcy might write to him, seek to explain himself by letter if not in person, begin, somehow, to repair their fractured relationship.

It was not lost on him the great sacrifice to his pride Richard had made by calling at Netherfield, and Darcy had hurried him out again without even giving him a chance to explain. For there must be some explanation, he realised that now. Perhaps he had mistaken what he had seen between his cousin and George Wickham. Richard was not fool enough to trust the man, not after all that had happened between them.

"You do look a little pale," Georgiana remarked, in a sharp tone, her eye blazing with annoyance that Darcy still refused to voice his opinion and instead left all the work of persuasion to her. "I think it only proper we go back to Netherfield and leave calling anywhere until tomorrow."

This was enough to jerk Bingley out of his stupor and he straightened, looking first at Georgiana and then Darcy, his brows knitting with confusion as he considered the explanation he had only half-heard.

"My brother is a little unwell," Georgiana offered, mercifully holding off from a second kick when Darcy hurriedly rearranged his features into a pathetic pallor. "And so I suggest we go straight home again." She stifled a yawn Darcy was not entirely sure was a fabrication. "I am tired, and I have no doubt you must be exhausted, for our journey from London was hurried." She laid a hand on Charles' arm and looked at him imploringly. "Don't let's call at Longbourn today. Better to leave it tomorrow, when we might be fresh and cheerful."

"Cheerful?" Charles was bitter. He scowled at the flowers that lay safely wrapped in paper on the seat opposite him. "I wish to get to the bottom of things. To find out for myself if Jane still cares."

"Of course. And you will." Georgiana paused, frowning a little while her mind hurried to think up an alternative course of action that might persuade Charles Bingley to obedience. "You might write a note, and send it with the flowers. It is kinder to prepare her for an interview, don't you think?"

Darcy held his breath, marvelling at his ingenue sister's ability to so manoeuvre the hearts and minds of gentlemen. Had Georgiana always been so cunning? *Or is it a skill she learned from her dalliance with George Wickham?* He was a little unnerved, even though he knew she worked for good in this instance and was succeeding far better than he would at managing Charles's mood.

"I might write her a note." Charles nodded, slowly, as if coming to see the wisdom in this plan. "And send the flowers on ahead." He paused. "Yes, I think - I think that would be best. We can call tomorrow, and then she will have had time to consider her answer. I do not wish to put her on the spot."

He glanced up at Darcy, looking a little like his old self once more.

"You do look pale, Darcy. I hope you aren't coming down with something."

"I am sure I will recover myself with a quiet evening at home," Darcy said, struggling not to smile at the expert way Georgiana had managed things.

"You will help me write to her, Georgie, won't you?" Bingley turned to her, his voice trembling with hope. "She must understand - I must make her understand - what she means to me. It was only because she did not know it, I'm sure..."

"If you want my help." Georgiana blushed, looking away from him quickly and Darcy frowned, wondering if he saw what he fancied he saw in his sister's blue eyes.

"I don't suppose I should blame Colonel Fitzwilliam," Bingley remarked, after a moment of tense silence had settled once more over the carriage. "After all, I wished to marry Jane the first moment I laid eyes on her. I can hardly blame him for feeling the same. And if he did not know -"

"Precisely!" Georgiana said, quickly. She darted a hopeful smile in Darcy's direction before throwing all her weight behind this way of thinking. "It is all a confusion of poor timing, I am sure of it. Nothing that cannot be remedied." She smiled. "We will begin as soon as we get home to Netherfield so that the flowers might be sent at once. And then we shall put the matter by and try to enjoy our evening." She bit her lip. "Perhaps Caroline can be persuaded to play for us."

"I should much rather you play," Bingley remarked, smiling a little guiltily at such a show of partiality. "Although you mustn't say so to Caroline."

"We might play a duet," Georgiana said, with more loyalty to the absent Miss Bingley than she perhaps deserved.

"A duet." Bingley nodded, smiling once more at Georgiana before turning to peer out of the window at the passing scenery.

Georgiana's eyes strayed to Darcy's and a wordless conversation took place between brother and sister.

*Another crisis averted*, her tentative smile said. *For now.*

PEACE REIGNED OVER the Longbourn parlour until the clattering of two pairs of feet thundered along the corridor and Lydia and Kitty burst together through the door, shrieking over one another in the excitement to share their news.

"We have just come from Meryton!" Kitty yelped. "We ran home because - because -" She hiccupped, trying to catch her breath and Lydia seized the opportunity to be the one to deliver their announcement.

"Mr Bingley has returned to Netherfield!"

Their words were so unexpected, and their arrival so chaotic, that it took a full minute before anybody could respond. Eventually, it was Mary who spoke, suspicion lacing her voice.

"Where did you hear this? Are you sure it's true?"

"Of course it is true!" Lydia retorted, with a toss of her head.

"Why should we invent such a thing?" Kitty was hurt. "Maria Lucas told us, and she heard it from her father. We thought Jane would want to know."

Jane bit down hard on her lip. She had managed, somehow, to hear this news without displaying any kind of reaction, but now that every eye turned towards her she felt the strain of remaining impassive.

"Why should Jane care so much to know it?" Elizabeth asked, desperately. She glanced with concern at her sister and then threw herself into the breach, taking at least some of their family's curiosity onto herself. "If it is true then it is of interest to all of us. Was not Mr Bingley a friend to our whole family?"

Lydia smirked.

"I merely thought the one member of this family who anticipated marrying him -"

"Oh, do be quiet, Lydia!"

This censure was so sharp and sudden and from the unlikely lips of Mrs Bennet, that Lydia recoiled as if she had been struck, bursting into noisy tears and fleeing from the room as hurriedly as she had entered it. When nobody immediately followed her, eager to pet and comfort, a wail reached the room demanding her sister.

"I must go," Kitty said, evidently unwilling to leave the room for fear she might miss some delicious gossip, but also knowing that to avoid Lydia in her moment of need would be to store up trouble for herself later. With a reluctant sigh, she shuffled after her sister.

"Jane?" Mrs Bennet, who was sitting next to Jane, clenched her hand tightly. "Jane, dear. You need not bear this shock alone. We are all here for you."

"Thank you, Mama," Jane said, stiffly. She tried to extricate her hand from her mother's crushing grip and smiled when she finally succeeded. "But truly you need not fret. I am - I am glad Mr Bingley is here. How pleasant it will be for Mr Darcy to have company again. I am sure..." She paused, taking a breath and praying her voice sounded more natural to her sisters' ears than it did to her own. "I am sure Charles hardly thinks of me at all." She did not say *and even if he did, it would not matter, for I am engaged to another man.* She was not even sure she could think those words truthfully in the quiet confines of her mind. Oh, why did Charles have to return at all! And why do so now?

"Did he say as much to you about his plans, Mary? When you met them in London?" Elizabeth asked, turning desperately to her sister. Jane could sense her concern and wished to reassure her that it was unnecessary but she knew, of everyone, that it was Lizzy who she would struggle most to persuade that she remained quite well and undisturbed by Charles Bingley's reappearance.

"Why should he have confided anything at all to Mary?" Mrs Bennet queried, dismissively. Her eyes brightened and she leaned forward, her eagerness to comfort her eldest daughter not quite outweighing her interest in potential gossip. She was not unlike her younger daughters in her thirst for drama.

"What will you say to him, if he calls here, Jane?" She frowned. "I suppose we might refuse to see him, although -"

"Mama, no!" Jane was more shocked by this than by the fact of Charles's return. Fact, for she knew that however vindictive her youngest sisters could be to others, even they would not go as far as to construct this story. Charles was back at Netherfield, no doubt with his sister in tow. If they were to remain then she must grow used to seeing him again. *At least until Colonel Fitzwilliam and I are married.*

She had not thought very much about the future after the wedding but now she could not help but consider it. Where would they live? Who would their friends be? Marriage to Charles Bingley, which she had dreamt of so fervently, had afforded her the hope of staying near home. She could be mistress of Netherfield Park, and the same friends and neighbours she had known all her life would be her friends, still. Her family would always be close. As wife to Colonel Richard Fitzwilliam...who knew?

*It is not an accurate comparison*, she reminded herself. *Charles never did care for me. I must stop deceiving myself into thinking he did. His return is a coincidence, only.*

At least, with Kitty and Lydia's eagerness to share gossip, she was afforded a little warning before he came to call. He would, she felt sure of it, and she must be mistress of her emotions before he did. She stood, so suddenly that every eye again fixed on her.

"Excuse me. I think I will go upstairs."

By some miracle, she managed to cross the short distance from her chair to the doorway without faltering, but she leaned heavily on the bannister as she climbed the stairs to her bedroom and when she closed the door firmly behind her, she leaned against it, hot tears welling in her eyes.

Why could Charles Bingley not have come home sooner? If she'd known he would come back she might have waited, mightn't she? Or had she made the decision she always would have made? Colonel Fitzwilliam was the same good man he had been when she consented to marry him. He loved her just as much now as he had then, and she cared equally for him. The presence of Charles Bingley at Netherfield Park changed absolutely nothing. Did it?

# Chapter Fourteen

"Jane? Jane, dear!"

Lizzy knocked a second time, then a third on her sister's bedroom door. She made her voice soft, as gentle as if she was trying to coax a kitten down from a tree.

"Jane?"

Her sister's answer, when it came, was thick and muffled, and Lizzy could not tell if that was because of tears or because Jane had buried herself under a pillow.

"Leave me alone."

Tempted to ignore Jane's instruction, Lizzy's fingers itched to turn the doorknob, but she drew her hand back before they even grazed its edge. *Let Jane be awhile*, she counselled herself, knowing how little she appreciated being disturbed when she was busy making sense of something.

And there must be a kind of sense to all this, surely?

Turning on her heel, Lizzy stalked back downstairs to the parlour, where Lydia and Kitty had crept back to join their mother and Mary, all discussing Mr Bingley - and Jane's sudden departure from the room - in hushed whispers.

"She won't come back downstairs," Lizzy declared, throwing herself down in agitation on the settee opposite the rest of her family.

"Poor dear." Mrs Bennet clucked her tongue but Lizzy could tell that at least some small degree of her sympathy masked disappointment at being denied a chance to speculate further with her eldest daughter about the meaning behind her former beau's sudden return.

Lizzy sighed, turning her attention to Lydia.

"How came you to know of Mr Bingley's return, anyway? I know you said Maria told you, but she is as inclined as anyone to make up such a story just to have something to gossip about."

Kitty gasped at Lizzy's cruel words but Lydia met her accusations without faltering.

"She heard it from her father." She jutted out her chin in a silent, defiant *so there* that she thought would silence Lizzy entirely.

"And he heard it from...?"

"Mr Bingley himself." This was Lydia's triumph, and she delivered it with a smile. "He crossed paths with Mr Bingley, Mr Darcy and Mr Darcy's sister who have all come to stay at Netherfield."

"Georgiana too?"

This was Mary, whose delight at being reunited with her friend from London was undeniable.

"What is she like, Mary?" Kitty asked, leaning forward and directing her attention to her sister. "Maria did not say much, but it may be that she did not know much. You are friends with Miss Darcy. Is she very pretty?"

Mary frowned, opening her mouth to say something about how she did not see what Miss Darcy's appearance had to do with her value as a person and as a friend, but Lizzy's attention remained fixed on Lydia.

"Then Mr Darcy must have known about it."

It was not a question, more a matter of her voicing a thought she could hardly bear entertaining.

"I dare say it was his idea!" Lydia replied, with a scornful smile. "You know that their retreat to London was at his suggestion. This return surely is, too. I wonder if he knows what damage his decision has done to poor Jane!"

Lizzy drew in a breath, nursing Lydia's words as tenderly as if they had been her own. Did Darcy know what he had done by encouraging Charles to return? He must have some inkling. And what of poor Colonel Fitzwilliam? If Jane was tormented by the return of a man she had once hoped to marry, what must he be thinking?

*How cruel to do such a thing to his own cousin! It isn't true. It can't be.*

"...Mr Darcy and his sister are very close," Mary was saying, with no small degree of pride at successfully making an audience of her whole family and having some intelligence to share that was welcomed. "I am sure that he missed her and that is why he invited her to join him at Netherfield."

Lizzy's brow sank into a scowl. There was no denying it, then. Darcy was responsible for creating the mess that now swirled all around them. Poor Jane! Poor Colonel Fitzwilliam! *And poor Mr Bingley!* If he cared at all, and Lizzy still could not decide which side of the argument for or against his caring she ought to come down on, then he would surely be hurt by the swift and absolute change in Jane's affections. *Even if he left her first, perhaps his return signifies that he did still care for her after all.* She reached a hand up to massage the frown-lines that were forming on her forehead. Oh, what a confusion this all was! *And Darcy is to blame for all of it!*

This, perhaps, rankled worst of all. Lizzy had fancied she knew Mr Darcy, had imagined she did, in any case. Had the version of him she had created in her mind been false all along? She had believed his claims, believed his good intentions. That very morning they had walked together and he had made no mention of the catastrophe he was inviting back to Meryton. He had sought to deceive her, which was worse than remaining aloof. *I might have considered him proud and rude and a whole host of other things, but never deceitful.* Now she wondered if she had known him at all, or merely seen two different faces he chose to wear. And why? Why not ever be himself?

There was a knock at the door that disrupted Lizzy's thoughts and Mary's treatise on the many virtues of Georgiana Darcy, and a servant stepped in, clutching a bouquet of beautiful, hot-house flowers.

"For Miss Bennet," he said, placing the vase that held them down on a table for a moment. "Ought I to take them upstairs?"

"No, leave them here," Mrs Bennet said, her eyes fixed on the bouquet. The servant retreated, closing the door behind him, and everyone was on their feet in an instant. Lizzy was quickest, snatching the card from where it lay nestled amidst the blooms and holding it out of reach of Lydia's eager, grasping hand.

"We oughtn't to read it," Mary began, but she was soon silenced by three sharp voices.

"It is only so that we might know who sent them," Lizzy explained, hurriedly opening the note and scanning it for a signature. She tried not to read its contents, but her eyes caught one or two words.

*Unchanged affections...understand...must speak to you...*
*C. B.*

*Charles Bingley!* Lizzy thought, folding the note and slipping it carefully into her sleeve.

"Lizzy!" Lydia wailed.

"What did it say?" Pragmatic Kitty cared little to see the actual note if she might yet be privy to its contents.

"I did not read it!" Elizabeth said, airily. It was only partly a lie. "I only looked at the signature." She turned to the flowers, fluffing them unnecessarily with one hand. "They are from Mr Bingley."

This caused a riot of whispered speculations to blow through the parlour like a gale, and Lizzy took the opportunity of her family's gleeful distraction to slip, unseen, through the door and scramble quietly back upstairs to Jane's room. She knocked gently on the door, then stooped and fed the folded note carefully through the gap between the bottom of the door and the floorboards.

"Mr Bingley sent flowers. I rescued his note before the girls could lay hold of it and thought you would wish to see it."

There was no answer from Jane, but after a moment's pause, the creak of a floorboard and the snatched disappearance of the note suggested she had retrieved it. Even now, she would be reading it. What would her reaction be?

Lizzy bit her lip, her heart full of concern for her sister and Colonel Fitzwilliam, and full of reproach for herself for being so instrumental in matching them. *I oughtn't to have encouraged Jane to care again*, she thought, wondering if she was to blame for the conflict that must be rending her poor sister's heart in two. She drew in a sharp breath, actively redirecting her blame towards the absent figure who deserved it more than she did. *And Mr Darcy ought not to have interfered - again! - in my sister's happiness.*

Her own heart was conflicted in this. She had almost believed she cared for Mr Darcy. How could she when his actions were so unfathomable? *I was mistaken,* she told her disbelieving heart. *I do not care. I could not. He is responsible for all the suffering my sister endures, and I will never forgive him for it!*

CANDLELIGHT FLICKERED warmly in the Netherfield parlour, making the shadows dance across the walls and the faces of his friends.

Yes, Darcy reasoned, it was the presence of his friends that contributed to the intangible warmth of the room. They had steered clear all evening of mentioning either Jane or Colonel Fitzwilliam again, and as a result, Charles seemed to have come a little back to life. Caroline, too, had rallied, appearing at dinner freshly dressed in what must have been a new dress that looked strangely out of place in the countryside but was objectively very becoming. She had been delighted with the suggestion of playing a duet with Georgiana and their first attempt had been so well-received after dinner that they were now halfway through their second, with a third and even a fourth lined up to follow.

There was a fumbling and a false note here and there and Darcy could not help but recall how perfectly matched

Georgiana and Mary's duets had been. It spoke to the closeness of their friendship, he supposed, which was in itself miraculous, considering how short a time the two had known one another.

*It is proof positive that* time known *is no true indicator of affection.* If only Darcy had fully appreciated that fact when first he had been in Meryton. He might have accepted the genuineness of Bingley's affections for Jane Bennet, instead of dismissing them as a fancy soon forgotten. *If I had not listened to Caroline, if I had not thought I knew better...*

What then? If he had not acted in accordance with Caroline Bingley he would not have encouraged the removal to London - which is not to say it would not still have happened for Caroline had a pronounced sway over her brother she was reluctant to give up, as she would be forced to do when he married. *Yet her influence was not enough to keep Charles from returning,* he reflected, again rueing his part in that particular development.

Jane had surely received the flowers that Charles had sent to Longbourn by now. What would her reaction be?

Darcy shifted uncomfortably in his seat, noticing that, despite Bingley's cheerful mood, his expression at rest was still cloudy and far-off, as if his thoughts, like Darcy's, lay elsewhere than the parlour he was sitting in. He, too, thought of Longbourn, Darcy did not doubt, and of the reception he might receive when he was permitted to call there.

Darcy sighed. He had no guarantee of a warm reception, himself. He was a prisoner, now, conscious that Longbourn was less open to him than it had been that very morning. Meryton, too, was a battleground, and he had held his breath the whole time that they were there, fearing to cross paths with either his cousin or George Wickham, and not knowing which he would prefer.

This was what rankled worst of all, he supposed. Did he owe Richard more by virtue of their family connection? Bingley's return to Meryton had the potential to destroy every hope Richard had of future happiness if Jane Bennet decided to break their engagement and favour Bingley once more.

*That is no reflection upon me,* he told himself. *It would be an indication of her inconstancy. In truth, it would prove that I was right all along to suspect her of being undeserving of my cousin.*

It was a hollow reflection and one that made his features sink into a scowl. Had he dared to sit in judgment of people who did not act precisely as he thought right? And what right did he have to judge anybody when his own actions were so open to criticism. *You caused this,* his conscience reminded him. He need not have written encouraging Bingley to return. He might have downplayed everything. *Or you might have been honest.* He squirmed. He could have - should have - written to Bingley insisting that it was too late. Jane had not only an affection with Richard Fitzwilliam but the pair were to be married and it was in Bingley's best interests to stay away, to try to move on. Charles might have disregarded him and come back to Meryton anyway, but at least Darcy's conscience would have been clear. Instead, it barracked at him whenever he was favoured with a moment's quiet thought. He was at odds with his cousin, made worse by his cruelty in summoning Charles Bingley back. And Elizabeth...

He sank deeper into his chair, resting his head in his hands. *Elizabeth will certainly never forgive me.* She held his previous interference in Jane's happiness against him: how much worse would this action damage their fragile peace? *Peace*. How much more he longed for from Elizabeth Bennet than a mere cessation of hostilities. He had glimpsed it, that morning, the fleeting hope that a future between them might be possible. He did love her so very much...and again, he had hesitated too long in saying so. Now it was surely too late, and in lashing out at his cousin, he had ruined his own chances at happiness...

"William?"

Georgiana's voice trilled with laughter and Darcy straightened, glancing around him in surprise to see that the gathered occupants of the parlour were staring at him in veiled, expectant amusement. He realised, at last, that his sister and Caroline had reached the end of their piece, and when they turned to their audience expecting praise, they had received acknowledgement only from Charles, as Darcy looked more like he was drifting towards sleep.

"Wonderful," he said, with forced brightness. He shifted in his seat, leaning forward and eyeing the piano with eagerness. "You will play another?"

"Only if you promise to listen and not fall asleep!" Georgiana smiled, selecting a piece with a faster tempo to ensure they did not lose their audience a second time.

# Chapter Fifteen

Jane woke early. She was not sure what time she had eventually succumbed to sleep, and the tray she had requested to take her evening meal on - to avoid the scrutiny of her sisters and parents - lay untouched in one corner of her room. She rubbed her eyes, blinking in the hazy near-dark, and fumbled to dress and descend downstairs in search of a cup of tea. That would make everything right again, she knew.

Longbourn was quiet. Even the servants moved so quietly as to avoid disturbing the rest of the house and Jane slipped unnoticed into the parlour, standing as close as she dared to the fireplace to absorb any warmth she could from the meagre coals that smoked there. Almost without meaning it, her eyes strayed to an ostentatious bunch of flowers perched on a side-table and she knew without needing to be told that these were the flowers Charles Bingley had sent. She frowned, recalling the letter Lizzy had slipped under her door. She had read it through, somehow committing it to memory, and she recalled it as she ran a finger over the wide petals of a rose that looked too perfect to be real.

*He still loves me.* The thought ought to have cheered her, made her heart lift. Instead, it made her stomach sink to the very floor. Once, she would have given anything to receive flowers like this from Charles Bingley, and could never have imagined the note that accompanied them. But they had come too late. He had returned too late. She had found love with someone else. *And I am happy with my decision.*

However often she repeated this fact to herself she still struggled to believe it. Was it possible that her feelings could change so swiftly and so completely? How well did she know Colonel Fitzwilliam?

*And do you know Charles Bingley any better?* She grew annoyed with herself, lamenting her indecision. If only she could be like Lizzy, who was so forthright in her opinions, entirely well-acquainted with her own mind.

"Jane?"

It was as if thinking of her sister had summoned her from the shadows, for with a whisper and a smile, Lizzy tiptoed into the parlour, crossing the room quickly to join Jane before the feeble fire.

"Did I wake you?" Jane asked, dully. She snatched her hand away from the flowers, hoping her sister had not noticed her fixation with them. "I tried to be quiet."

"You were a ghost!" Lizzy said, shivering a little and hunching so close to the fire that she almost stepped on it. "But you know me. I am perennially early to rise."

"Then you will prefer privacy," Jane wagered, tugging her shawl a little tighter around her shoulders. "I won't disturb you."

"You don't!" Lizzy hissed, grabbing a tight hold of Jane's arm and bidding her stay where she was. "And you needn't leave. I have been aching to speak to you and now, at last, we have an opportunity." She peered past Jane towards Mr

Bingley's flowers. "You must tell me what is on your mind, dearest Jane. I can only imagine how conflicted you must feel."

"Can you?" Jane's voice still sounded so flat and unlike its usual self that she grimaced, wishing she was better at concealing her true feelings. "I scarcely know how I feel."

Lizzy nodded, biting her lip.

"Then you still care..."

"I don't know!" Jane's response was louder than she meant it to be, and she shot a wary glance to the ceiling, but the rest of the house remained mercifully still, silent and sleeping and undisturbed by her outburst. Taking care to moderate her tone to a whisper, she turned back to Elizabeth. "It does not matter, anyway. I have consented to marry Colonel Fitzwilliam. I will marry Colonel Fitzwilliam."

"And you...love Colonel Fitzwilliam?" Lizzy ventured, evidently hoping for an answer in the affirmative that Jane found herself strangely unable to give.

"This is all Darcy's fault!" Lizzy's eyes darkened malevolently, and Jane's despair turned to confusion.

"How...?"

"He summoned Bingley back here! I know it is his doing. He sought to separate you from Charles Bingley in the first instance and now he seeks to part you from his cousin. He is a villain, a scoundrel, a -"

"But I thought you cared for him?" Jane shook her head. "You cannot mean half the things you say. Of course Mr Darcy is not to blame for this. Lizzy, this is nobody's fault. It is an accident of fate, and one we must live with. I have made my decision and I -"

Her voice trailed off. *I do not regret it*, she might have said. *I am happy with it*. Neither seemed entirely true.

"I will abide by it."

It was strangely formal and entirely unpersuasive if the uncomfortable set of Elizabeth's lips was anything to judge by. In the shadows, her hand found Jane's and squeezed, tightly, a silent show of sisterly encouragement.

"He is a good man," Lizzy said, loyal to the last. "Colonel Fitzwilliam is a good man and a kind one. He adores you." She swallowed. "And he would never allow the opinions of his friends to sway him from his heart's desire."

There. Lizzy had cast her lot in with Richard's and made her stance perfectly clear. She would support her sister in marrying him and oppose any attempt to separate them. *She is placing herself in opposition to Charles Bingley, then.* Jane drew a breath. *And, if her suspicion about him is right, she opposes Mr Darcy too.* Her heart sank, fearing that, whatever decision she made, it was not merely her future that hung in the balance, but Lizzy's too.

"I'm hungry," Elizabeth announced, seeking to distract Jane from her concerns if she could not allay them completely. "Let's take some breakfast. Everything will look a little brighter after some food and drink."

Jane did not object, allowing her sister to lead her to the breakfast room as gently as if she was a child. If only she could surrender her will entirely to Elizabeth, allow her sister to make greater decisions than merely what to eat and drink. How easy life would be!

She frowned, thinking that there was a way she could do just that. She paused, as they reached the table, tugging Lizzy to a stop and forcing her to look at her.

"Do you prefer Colonel Fitzwilliam?" she asked, desperately. "Do you think I make the right decision in marrying him?"

Lizzy did not answer straight away, and Jane watched the shadows that danced across her features carefully, trying to deduce their true meaning before at last, Lizzy spoke, quietly and confidently and with all the certainty Jane lacked.

"I think you will know the right decision if you look to your heart. This is not something that mere logic can decide for you. Since when has love ever been logical?"

Jane nodded, her heart sinking further to the ground. If only love was logic. If only she could make a decision and not regret it, or second-guess it, or have it complicated by other people.

*I do care for Richard Fitzwilliam. He is so kind, so pleasant and amiable and good. And I know he cares for me. But...I fear I do not love him. Not the way that I love Charles Bingley. Oh! Whatever shall I do?*

RICHARD'S APPREHENSION grew with every step he took. His path was quite familiar now. Enough that he could find his way in his sleep, he supposed. It was a good thing, for his thoughts were entirely occupied as he walked, so that he came within sight of Longbourn long before he was aware of it.

*Well*, he thought, slowing his pace as he approached the house. *Here I am.* He paused to adjust his uniform, which, while always smartly to code, he had taken particular care with that morning. It suited him well, he knew, and he straightened to the fulness of his height, wishing, with a grimace, that he were a little more handsome. *It does not matter*, he told himself, remembering that even Charles Bingley, for all his charm and wealth, was not remarkably well-looking. He winced as he looked at the small bouquet of wildflowers he had procured on his way out of Meryton. He had clutched them too tightly as he walked, venting a little of his anxiety on the poor posy, which now looked a little wilted and unwell. He checked his pocket-watch, reassuring himself that, whilst early, it was not *too* early to call at a house which had become almost a second home to him. There was no need to feel such anxiety and yet his heart fluttered in his chest as he knocked at the front door and it was not without effort that he managed to rearrange his features into a smile that appeared more cheerful than he felt.

"Good morning!" He greeted the servants warmly and was welcomed easily into the parlour, which comfortably contained above half of the family.

"Colonel Fitzwilliam!" Mrs Bennet was the first to greet him, ushering him in to join them. "We did not expect you!" Her broad smile faltered a little as she turned to Jane, who was seated beside her. "Did we?"

"We didn't," Jane said, her eyes dancing to Richard for only a moment before sliding away again. "Although it is a lovely surprise to see you."

*A surprise?* Richard blinked, his smile slipping. Was it truly a surprise, when he could be found here at Longbourn almost as often as he could be found anywhere else. Jane still did not look at him, and Richard wondered, anxiously, whether the surprise of his presence that morning was a particularly welcome one.

"These are for you." Lacking any other greeting and hoping that the presentation of a gift would be enough to secure Jane's fleeting attention at last, he thrust the bouquet forward.

"Oh, how lovely!" Mrs Bennet nudged Jane, none too subtly, and she looked up at last, her lips stretching in a pained smile as she reached for the posy that looked rather small and weedy, now that Richard looked at them again.

"You are very kind," she said. "I will find a vase for them." She looked almost without meaning to at the sideboard and Richard followed her gaze, a little taken aback by an ostentatiously rich bouquet that dwarfed both the vase that struggled to contain it and his own meagre offering.

"Ah -" he began, fumbling for some words to dismiss his gift, to take back the posy and dispose of it, substituting some different, better gift. Jane had brushed past him before he could summon a word, though, and he was left in the strange silence that followed in her wake. Clearing his throat, he turned to Mrs Bennet, nodding briefly at Elizabeth, who was sitting next to her. "What beautiful flowers. You have excellent taste, Mrs Bennet."

"Oh, they are not my flowers!" Mrs Bennet giggled. "They are -"

"Mine!" Lizzy blurted, desperately shooting her mother a look that Richard did not miss, nor misunderstand. "But I know Jane has always much preferred wildflowers to those that are grown in a hot-house. Your gift was very kind, Colonel Fitzwilliam."

There was a forced friendliness to Elizabeth's voice and Richard felt his heart sink bitterly into his stomach.

"I did not like to come empty-handed," he ventured. "Not when -"

Before he could say more, the door opened, but it was not merely Jane returning with a vase, as he had suspected. No, it was not Jane at all, but Lydia, red-faced and breathing heavily as if she had come running in from outside, and she beamed, victoriously escorting visitors of her own.

"Look who Kitty and I found outside!" she declared, leading a procession of Mr Darcy, Mr Bingley, Miss Bingley and Georgiana.

Everyone stared at each other in silent horror, and it was at that moment that Jane chose to return, the colour draining from her face as she looked from Richard to Charles Bingley and back again.

"I - " Her grip on the vase weakened and by some miracle Lizzy leapt forward at the last minute to take it from her, stowing it safely on the side, in the shadow of the larger bouquet and gently guiding her sister to a chair with a grace and familiarity Richard wished he had thought to offer.

"Well!" Mrs Bennet stuttered, gesturing around her. "What a great number of guests! And all at once! How...how charming. Do, do sit down, won't you?"

At first, nobody moved, but eventually, Darcy shuffled to one side, seeking the comfort of a quiet, shadowy corner in which to hide, Richard supposed. His movement allowed Georgiana the freedom to bolt forward, and she did, right towards her cousin, with a radiant smile.

"Richard! I was hoping we might see you, although I never dreamed it would be here!"

"Aye? And why should I not call here?" Richard could hear the bitter note in his voice and fought to clear it, but it was not easily done. "Is it so very unexpected that a gentleman should call on his fiancée?"

Bingley cleared his throat at Richard's use of the word *gentleman*, a pointed protest that served only to inflame Richard's anger all the more. He shook off Georgiana's hand and turned to face her companions, his gaze narrowing as he met Charles Bingley.

"I am surprised to find you calling here, and so early. Surely you are used to keeping London hours?"

"One needn't stand on ceremony when calling on one's friends, Colonel." Bingley gave him a toothy smile and Richard fought an urge to lash out at him. "Ah, I see my flowers arrived. I trust you received my note, as well?" He addressed his question to Jane, speaking brazenly as if they were the only two people in the room.

Richard's temper soared, but he somehow kept himself from saying a word. He could not keep himself from looking, though, and saw the way Jane flushed scarlet before slowly looking up and meeting Bingley's gaze. From his eyes, she did not immediately look away and Richard saw, in that one, tiny gesture, all his future hopes dissolve.

"It is good to see you, Richard," Georgiana said again, desperately speaking to fill the silence in hopes she might cut the tension that surely every person present could feel. "I wonder if you have no other obligations today, whether we might -"

"Actually, I have a great many obligations today," Richard muttered, shaking himself free of her grasp a second time and pushing past the crowd towards the door. "I oughtn't to have come at all, only -"

"You mustn't let us keep you from your tasks, Colonel Fitzwilliam," Bingley said, that same infuriating smile still on his face. His gaze travelled hypnotically back to Jane's. "It is time we were able to get a little reacquainted with old friends."

Richard froze in the doorway, staring with disbelief at Charles Bingley. The man was shameless and nobody - not Darcy, not Georgiana, not even Jane - seemed to notice or care the liberties he took speaking with such familiarity to a young woman who was another man's betrothed. It was infuriating and - worse - insulting. *And it shall not be borne.*

"Perhaps you will permit me a word or two before leaving," Ricard choked out, from between clenched teeth. "Outside?"

Bingley paused, his eyes sweeping the room. Something in him, some degree of bravado, was tempted to goad Richard into speaking here and now, in a roomful of witnesses, but at last he relented with a slight nod.

"Very well."

Richard bowed stiffly and retreated, his ears tuned to Bingley's footsteps behind him. It was time he did what he ought to have done long ago. If Charles Bingley was determined to encroach on Richard's territory and force some imagined claim to Jane Bennet's heart, then he deserved to be held to account. *And may the best man win.*

# Epilogue

"You must go after them!"

In the wake of Mr Bingley's and Colonel Fitzwilliam's silent departure, an icy silence had settled over the parlour, until Elizabeth Bennet was the one to break it. She looked at her sister, first, whose cheeks reddened but who kept her gaze fixed on the floor. Next, Elizabeth's gaze swept from Georgiana to Caroline before hopelessly resting on Darcy's. He was not quick enough to look away. No, it was not a matter of speed. How could he look away from those eyes that were fixed on him with desperation?

"Will you do nothing?"

"Very well." All at once, life seemed to flood back into Darcy's still limbs, and he turned on his heel, stalking after his friends and fearing to come across a brawl that would need a physical intervention. He tugged at his collar, loosening his cravat and was moments from tugging his cuffs free, too, before he saw that Charles and Richard had not come to blows. *Yet.*

"You cannot be serious." Richard scoffed. "You truly think you have the upper hand in this? You act without shame -"

"I have no need for shame!" Charles sniffed. "I knew Jane Bennet long before you ever even arrived in Hertfordshire."

"Yes, and she pledged herself to me shortly after you left. I do not see what bearing your knowing one another beforehand has to do with this."

"You cannot truly think she cares for you?" Charles scoffed. "If she accepted your proposal -"

"She did accept it. We are to be married, and you shall cease in your campaign to seduce -"

"I sent flowers, Fitzwilliam. It is hardly a seduction for the ages. If a bunch of flowers is all it takes -"

"Gentlemen," Darcy spoke quietly, but even so his voice seemed to have a calming effect on his friends. Momentarily, at least. Both Richard and Charles turned to glare at him, and Darcy wished he could be anywhere but here. This, then, was the position had tried to avoid. The position fate had placed him in. He was caught between his friend and his cousin and there would be no way to placate them both.

"Ah, Darcy you are just in time. Your cousin here has just challenged me to a duel."

"I asked you to abandon your nonsense, or be made to abandon it," Richard retorted, his eyes flashing dangerously. "If you choose to perceive that as being called out -"

"I do not intend to solve the matter with a brawl here and now, if that is your alternative suggestion," Charles said, with a regal sniff. "I do not know how matters tend to be resolved *in the regiment.*"

He spoke with such scornful disdain for Richard, for his position in the militia, for everything his cousin valued and took pride in that Darcy himself winced. It was the sort of unremitting pride he, himself, might previously have exhibited and it garnered just the result it might have been expected to, from one such as Colonel Richard Fitzwilliam.

"I do not need to be lectured on the rites and rituals of being a gentleman by the son of a tradesman." His eyes narrowed. "Very well. Dawn, then. Name your place."

Bingley conjured a name with such speed and efficacy that Darcy was left certain he had been considering the matter long before this moment, planning it out in his head.

Richard's head dipped in the tiniest nod of acquiescence, his gaze sliding over to Darcy, who opened his mouth to say something -anything - that might ease the situation.

"Darcy will be my second," Charles said, quicky, and Darcy saw the small window he might have had to influence things towards calm slam shut. His cousin's eyes narrowed, his features slipping into an unreadable mask. "Do you have someone you can ask -"

"I have someone in mind," Richard said, briskly returning his gaze to Charles. "You need not spare a concern for my ability to fight a duel and win. The last time I held a weapon is, I wager, rather more recent than yours." He turned on his heel and stalked away, leaving Charles and Darcy to stare after him.

"Well." Charles turned, looking almost pleased with himself. "Come, Darcy, let's go back inside. We shan't let this moment of unpleasantness spoil a social call. The ladies have surely missed us."

*The ladies* might have missed them, but only one lady stood as if to guard the door to the parlour. She let Charles enter with only a slight frown, which descended into a look of absolute dislike as she moved to block the doorway to Darcy.

"A duel?"

"You heard." Darcy swallowed, raking a hand through his dark hair and wondering how it was Elizabeth Bennet still managed to see as if to his very soul. "Did everyone...?"

"They were too busy talking." She waved away his concern, and took a step towards the window, motioning to him to follow her in hopes that their few shared words might likewise go unnoticed by the rest of the house. "Jane will be devastated if she discovers it, so you must find a way to stop it."

"Stop it?" Darcy shook his head. "Stop it how? The best I can do is go along with it and ensure nobody gets killed."

"That is the most ridiculous thing I ever heard!" Elizabeth's face went white at the word *killed* and for the most fleeting of moments, Darcy dared to hope she spared at least a little of her concern for him. Her gaze flashed with fear and anger and he realised she was concerned not for him but despite him.

"What would you have me do instead?" he asked. "Leave them to fight it out between themselves with nary a person to moderate? As second I have a chance -"

"A chance to ensure the best man wins." Lizzy scowled. "I can't believe you would side against Colonel Fitzwilliam. He is your cousin! Don't you care about him at all? Or your friend? You care nothing for me and my family -"

"I care everything for you. And for your family. I acted rashly in writing to Charles but I never thought it would lead to this. I did not think - I did not think -"

"Well, now you must think," Lizzy said, sharply. "Think of a way out of this."

They were standing very close to one another now, so close that it seemed to Darcy nothing at all to take her hand in his, startled at how naturally their fingers fit together, as if they had been designed to do just that.

"Help me," he whispered, his voice softer now, his gaze tender, hopeful, seeing a way forward that might be possible only with her by his side, his helper, partner, friend. "Help me, Elizabeth. You are the only one who can."

*The End*

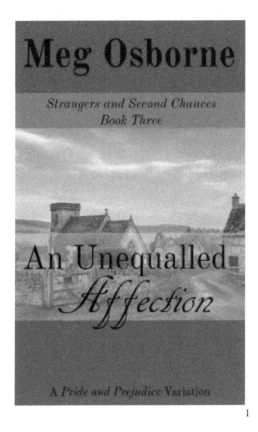

1

An Unequalled Affection[2]
Book Three[3]
*Available to Pre-order Now*[4]

---

1. https://books2read.com/u/brPqlk

2. https://books2read.com/u/brPqlk

3. https://books2read.com/u/brPqlk

4. https://books2read.com/u/brPqlk

## Why Not Try...?

When Fitzwilliam Darcy travels to Hertfordshire with his friend, the last person he expects to see is Elizabeth Bennet, the young woman who broke his heart in London four years previously...

---

Book 1 in a fun new Pride and Prejudice variation series. Romance and Reconciliation what if Mr Darcy and Elizabeth Bennet met long before the Meryton Assembly...?

# About the Author

Meg Osborne is an avid reader, tea drinker and unrepentant history nerd. She writes sweet historical romance stories and Jane Austen fanfiction, and can usually be found knitting, dreaming up new stories, or on twitter @megoswrites

Read more at www.megosbornewrites.com.

CPSIA information can be obtained
at www.ICGtesting.com
Printed in the USA
BVHW081828200421
605388BV00006B/638

9 781393 874416